Alongside Hamilton

My Unlikely Friendship With an Ivy League Athlete, High Society Bachelor, Roosevelt Rough Rider, American Hero

By Carson Cunningham

Imprint: Huckleberry Books

Alongside Hamilton: My Unlikely Friendship With an Ivy League Athlete, High Society Bachelor, Roosevelt Rough Rider, American Hero

ISBN: 978-0-9904945-3-9

Library of Congress Control Number: 2020948880

Copyright © 2021

Design by Baris Celik

Table of Contents

Chapter 1

May 1898, outskirts of *San Antonio.*

Hamilton Fish and I, and a bunch of other Rough Riders, were sitting on our horses, about to start drill. The sun blazed down, Texas-style, but the thousands of locals that had come out to watch us didn't seem to mind. Heat be damned, they were excited to get a look at us Rough Riders. We were a motley crew of men and, truth be told, the whole nation was talking about us.

We were dressed in full uniform: tan slouch hat, navy flannel and bandana, rugged khaki trousers, thick gloves, and boots. And we were fully armed. I'm sure we looked tough and rough-hewn, but I was scared stiff. I was seventeen and didn't really know a thing about war. It helped, though, to have Hamilton alongside.

Under the searing sun and with the crowd looking on, Lieutenant Colonel Teddy Roosevelt ordered us to charge up a hill. We spurred our horses forward, hootin' and hollerin', together making a powerful rumble. Within a matter of moments, however, our yelps turned to gasps as a young Mexican girl scampered out from the crowd. She'd done so quickly, just all of a sudden, and now she was right out in front of us. She looked upward as we bore down upon her, her face turning from a look of wonder to one of horror, her body seizing. *My God*, I thought to myself.

In that instant it was clear to all of us that getting our horses to stop before trampling her would be impossible. Still, I yanked my reins up with all my might, just like the other Rough Riders around me did. And I closed my eyes. I heard the crowd gasp and then, expecting the worst, I looked down. But lo and behold beneath me I saw only sun-scorched earth and horse legs. Confused, I pulled my gaze up. There I saw the young girl, with a look of wonder on her face, riding away from me, her chin resting on the shoulder of the man who had saved her—Hamilton Fish.

When Hamilton's save fully registered with the crowd, it roared with approval. And even beyond San Antonio, word of it spread quickly. Newspapers across the nation reported it with headlines like this: *Rough Rider, Coveted Bachelor, Athletic Standout, Member of America's Smart-set, Saves Girl.*

The papers explained that when the girl ran out in front of our horses, rather than carry out a futile attempt to pull up, Hamilton had spurred his horse ahead, hoping to get out in front of the other Rough Riders. With only a fraction of a second separating the young girl from death, he'd reached down and pulled her up to safety, like it was nothing. Journalists knew the public would love it: America's elite could be heroes. They were with the rest of us. They cared.

The night after the save, Hamilton and I went into town with a group of fellows, among them Woodbury Kane and Bill Tiffany. I'll get to them later. We started in on some poker—stud poker with wilds, I think it was—when by and by a lady came to our table. It was the mother of the young girl that Hamilton had saved.

"I'm so happy," she said, smiling. "All day, all over I look. And now, finally, I find you."

Hamilton stood up politely. "Sorry you went to all that trouble, ma'am. How can I help you?"

She seemed in awe as she looked at him. He could have that effect. He was six-foot-two, and strong, with broad shoulders and blue eyes, and the ladies loved his thick, light brown, curly hair. She stepped forward and hugged him. Then she reached into her pocket to pull out a pewter-based pendant with an image of St. Joseph on it. "Something I give you," she said. Hamilton took the pendant in hand. "My daughter, she wore this around her neck, ever since her papa gave it to her, at her baptism," the woman went on. "It protects against danger. I know you go to war. Please have this."

"Thank you," Hamilton said.

The mother hugged him again and started to walk away. Then she paused and said, "Don't lose. Otherwise, you will be in even more danger than before I give it to you."

"Thank you," he said again, bowing his head slightly.

The gesture moved him, but Hamilton wasn't Catholic, and he thought people truckled too much when it came to "superstition." So back at camp he pulled the pendant out of his pocket and said, "Rory Mac, you're Catholic. Here, have this."

"Thanks Ton," I said, calling him by his nickname.

Several nights later, while I was trying to get some shuteye on a train bound for Tampa, I overheard a group of Rough Riders talking about Ton's save of that young girl. These were hard-nosed westerners—wranglers and sharp-shooters, guys who knew great riding when they saw it—and they still couldn't believe what he had done.

It hadn't surprised me all that much, though. I'd seen Ton do amazing things before. Years earlier, he'd snatched me up from the clutches of despair not entirely unlike the way he'd saved that girl from the horses.

Chapter 2

Growing up in Ireland during the potato famine, my mom, Clair, didn't have much food or money. She didn't have much hope, either, except for when it came to America. Where she lived in Ireland, she mainly saw difficulty. She and her family scraped by to stay alive, just like the other families around them. In her teens she finally got her chance to go to America by boat. It was on her way over that she met my father, Willum, in steerage.

In Manhattan, my mom took care of the home. My dad worked as a butcher. They could get by, and things would likely have gone well for them, but the drink grabbed hold of my dad and never really let go. When I was eight years old, his liver gave out. I wish I remembered him better. I do know his death took a big part of my mom's soul. She never blamed him, though, and she never spoke poorly of him; she just grieved in her own quiet way.

Soon after he died, she went to work doing laundry. For hours on end, in a building basement with filthy, stagnant air, my mom and the other washerwomen would use lye soap and a rough washboard to rub clothes and bedding clean. Standing for most of the day, they worked with their hands and their backs. I spent more than a day or two working in the wash house, and it always led to some of the deepest sleep I ever had.

It didn't pay much, though. To help us get by, when I was about nine, I took to selling Joseph Pulitzer's *The World* in midtown Manhattan. Although folks didn't quite yet call them "yellows," *The World* was a "yellow" paper and it, and its sort, were already rocking the traditional moorings of the newspaper industry. It was happy chance, then, that I started to work in the business at perhaps the most exciting time in the history of American journalism.

To attract readers, papers like Pulitzer's *The World* and William Randolph Hearst's *New York Journal* printed news in colorful, hyperbolic fashion, focusing on stories that pierced the heart and stirred the imagination. They hired newsmen who saw themselves as story movers rather than detached commentators. This was journalism that acted. And they started price wars.

At first, the more traditional papers, like the *New York Sun* and the *Press*, tried to dismiss *The World* and the *Journal* as cheap and sensational. But when demand for the upstarts surged, it didn't take long for the old guard to start changing the content of their papers to better compete. For a time during this drawn-out drama the label "yellow" became a kind of badge of honor as folks began to truly understand just how much Pulitzer and Hearst had changed things.

Anyway, as I say, I was around nine years old when I learned to hawk newspapers, to belt out headlines just like the yellows printed them, to scrabble, to read people. Sure, newsboy work could be hard, but it taught me how to survive. It also led me to Ton Fish.

***

I remember the morning as clearly as it broke back then. I was on my best corner, Forty-ninth and Madison, right near the entrance to Columbia University, hollering away, "Hungry and Sick! Hungry and Sick! Read about the storms! The Gulf Ravaged! Hungry and Sick!" As loud as my voice might've been, the truth is that rather than talking about the folks in New Orleans, I could have been talking about myself. It'd been a rough several months for a lot of folks, what with the economic panic that ripped through the nation in 1893. Mom and I had felt it. Much of her laundry work had stopped and fewer papers sold, even at two cents for sixteen pages worth of news.

The day prior my cut of sales amounted to fourteen cents. That was the morning and evening editions combined, and that was only because I'd worked till midnight trying to sell the remnants of my last bundle. For several weeks, in our two-room, back-corner apartment on the top floor of the dumbbell-shaped tenement we lived in, we'd eaten mostly gruel, bread, and lard. Every now and then an old butcher friend of my late father—we called him "Chops"—would bring some meat to us, but his family was hurting, too. And it pained my mom to take the handout anyhow. She only allowed it on account of Chops having been a friend of my father.

At any rate, we were hungry and a bit sickly. But on this particular morning, a young man that I'd sold a paper to almost every day for the past few weeks did something unexpected. Perhaps he saw desperation on my face; maybe he noticed the tattered clothes hanging on my thin frame, or my callused, filthy bare feet. I never did ask him. Whatever it was, after he dropped a couple of copper pennies into my palm, picked up a copy of the *World*, looked me in the eye and said, "Thanks, newsie." He stopped himself before walking away, looked back toward me, pulled a paper-wrapped package out of his Prince Albert coat, and tossed it to me. I peeled away the wrapper to find sliced cheese and salami inside. My grin must've stretched to the Hudson. I was about to take a bite but then I remembered how my mom wouldn't approve of taking a handout, hungry as I was. I hesitated a moment, then held my hand out to give it back, and said, "Appreciate it, but I can't take handouts."

Ton didn't take the package back. He just looked at me for several moments, a little surprised, like he was taking measure of me. "Oh," he said. "Well, what if I've got some work I'd like to ask you about? Could we consider it a kind of payment to hear me out?"

"I suppose," I said, reopening the package and leaning in for a bite.

"What's your name?" he asked.

"Rory MacGregor, sir," I said between bites.

"Ah, don't call me sir," he said. "The name's Hamilton Fish."

"Well, thank you, sir…I mean, thank you, Hamilton."

"Rory MacGregor, huh?"

I nodded.

"About that work," he continued. "I need a pugilist's second, corner help for a bout I've got this Friday. You ever been a second?"

"Nope."

"It's not too hard; you'll pick it up quick."

"What's it pay, if you don't mind me asking?"

Ton thought about it for a moment. "How about I give you a buck?"

I nearly hit the ground. On a great day, selling papers might net me thirty cents. A whole dollar for an evening's work felt like darned near a fortune to me. I couldn't get the words out, so I shook my head up and down. Ton smiled and told me I could meet him right where we were, at the entrance to Columbia, at nine o'clock that Friday night.

***

I'd walked by McSorley's Ale House on East Seventh plenty of times, with its brick façade and green sign—a nod to the McSorley family's Irish roots—and I'd even peered through the establishment's windows on occasion. The place was a throwback. It served only two types of beer, light and dark. It had no chairs, just long wooden bars running along its walls, which is the way alehouses used to be. And they kept a poster on the wall from 1865 that asked for "information leading to the arrest of the assassin of Abraham Lincoln."

One thing I didn't know about McSorley's, though, was that it had an upstairs back room set up for boxing. This backroom was smoke-filled and dark, except for the ring in the center, upon which a light shone from the ceiling. Standing around the ring were men of all sorts, three and four deep, packed in tight. Swallowtails rubbed up against longshoremen, rough-looking manual laborers stood alongside Wall Street financiers. Ton shook hands with a few men just inside the secret entryway to the room. He had gotten ready for the bout in a small office down the second floor hall. I'd helped tape his hands there. Now I stood just behind the ropes about to watch Ton fight.

There's a peculiar tension in the air before a fight starts. I could feel it, and when the bell rang a rush of blood surged through me. Ton started in on his opponent with some quick jabs and used his feet to keep his opponent off balance. I hadn't expected to get invested in the bout so quickly. Soon I was pounding the canvas, hollering for Ton, which prompted a few fellas near me to start chuckling. I heard one of 'em ask, "How'd that kid even get in here?"

The fight followed the Queensbury rules. The gloves

they used, though, looked nothing like the pillows that fighters wear these days, which was no small matter, seeing as Ton's 225-pound opponent weighed about thirty pounds more than him. Three minutes in, the bell rang to end round one. I slid between the ropes onto the canvas with Ton's stool in hand, just like he'd told me to do. He sat on the stool, and I gave him his jug of "water." Well, he'd said it was water, but I'd tried a little myself and it burned like no water I'd ever tasted. He took a couple swigs.

"Give 'em all you got, Ton. I got a deuce riding on you," a guy from the crowd hollered.

"Manhattan's Corbett—put him down, Ton," another shouted.

Yet another said, "You're a bum, Ton, a wannabe Corbett. Stick with college, ya bum!"

Much like round one, in the second, Ton broke the big fellow down. He jabbed and moved, jabbed and countered, and then moved again. I knew little about the sport, but Ton's tactics felt methodical, scientific. I could sense the precision even if I didn't really know how to look for it quite yet. In round five, the big timber fell, and Ton won.

A rush of money changed hands in the crowd. By the time two fresh fighters had sauntered into the ring, Ton and I were heading back to the offices that doubled as staging areas for fighters. As I cut the tape off Ton's hands, a man stopped by to give him an envelope. Ton's cut of the pot, I presumed. The real payoff for Ton, though, was being in an arena in which background or privilege didn't matter—just performance.

Ton asked me if I'd like to meet up with a couple of his buddies at the downstairs bar. There, Ton and his Columbia friends talked about how the "smart" money had been against him. Just like when folks underestimated Gentleman Jim, one of them said.

We caught a streetcar bound for midtown and then walked to my tenement. Ton asked about home, who looked after me and such. I told him about my dad passing and how hard my mother worked. He was quiet for a stretch.

"You run a good corner, Rory. I like your moxie. How about this. How 'bout I pay you a dollar-twenty-five each fight, instead of a dollar, so long as you save that extra quarter, with the idea being that when winter's up you surprise your mother by taking her out to a fancy dinner?"

It sounded great to me.

Upon making it to my tenement house, Ton handed me a dollar twenty-five. "I fight again next month."

"I can't wait, Mr. Fish. Thank you."

"Call me Ton—and thank you."

I felt light walking up the several flights to our tenement. Not only did I have money to share with my mom, but I had someone to look up to. He went to college, and he could fight. He moved with ease in worlds I could only dream about. Somehow, I sensed that my life would never be the same.

Chapter 3

For folks used to automobiles, streetlights, modern plumbing, and lawfulness, the Manhattan of 1895 would seem unrecognizable. At that time, there were wagons and cable cars and thousands upon thousands of horse-drawn carriages but not a single stop sign, let alone a traffic light. There wasn't even a hard and fast law telling you which side of the street to drive on. European visitors couldn't believe it. And the plumbing, my goodness. Many of the tenements, mine included, only had outhouses in the "courtyard," and these outhouses, when coupled with the smell of horse droppings out on the streets, made for a rather foul neighborhood stench. At least my mom and I didn't have to sleep in shifts. A lot of folks did—they'd rent bunk space eight hours at a time. There were pig farms scattered about too, and enough horse manure to blanket the borough, or so it seemed.

At the same time, mid-1890s Manhattan was cutting edge. It had moving pictures and Berliners, which were early record players, a hotel with a long-distance telephone line, and Coca-Cola. It was the nation's capital for banking, finance, arts and entertainment, and it had the country's largest commercial port. There were architectural wonders and an elite class whose wealth was mind-boggling. Still, among its two million inhabitants, there was more horse thievery, gambling, political corruption, and prostitution than anywhere else in America. Taken altogether, New York City was a mishmash of old and new, poor and rich, immigrant and native, pig farmer and banker, the likes of which the world had never seen before.

My world, the tenements of Hell's Kitchen, rarely

converged with Ton Fish's, the East Village and Kips Bay areas—unless you knew someone from school whose mom did the wash or cooked for a family like his. That's why for me catching a break from him was such a big deal.

***

In the several months I spent as Ton's second, he fought several bouts. He was victorious in all except for one. The loss was to a guy darn near fifty pounds heavier. And even then Ton wouldn't go down until what seemed like a sledgehammer was brought down upon his head.

Groggy and bloodied in the staging area, he looked up at me. "Old boy, we almost got that heavy, didn't we?"

It made me mighty sore to see him busted up like that, but he didn't seem to mind the pain. He liked the training and being in the arena. If he went idle for too long, he'd get to feeling restless and antsy. Over time I came to learn that, win or lose, his boxing, everything about it—the willpower, the strategy, the brutal competitiveness, the pain—helped him feel whole and satisfied, at least for a little while.

On the night he lost to the heavy, Ton and I hopped off a streetcar near Thirty-ninth street and met up with his friend Pat. As we stepped to the side of the Old Met, a splendid horse-drawn carriage—the kind my mom liked to read about in the *World's* society section, the kind of carriage most folks never got to actually see up close—pulled up alongside a discreet side door. A couple of minutes later, a woman, with the unmistakable round face and dark hair of *the* Mrs. Astor, stepped out of this Old Met side door. She had what must've been twenty diamonds dangling from her neck. I stared as a liveried servant helped Mrs. Astor climb into her waiting carriage.

When it pulled away, another carriage, almost as nice, took its place. Moments later three beautiful, elegantly dressed women walked through the same door. They were tall and well put-together, their hair immaculately done, jewels seemingly everywhere. The one with wavy brunette hair and dark brown eyes was most striking. I watched as Ton and Pat greeted the ladies and escorted them to the waiting carriage. *They actually know these women*, I thought to myself.

We joined them inside the carriage, and it pulled away. The tall brunette with dark eyes, Victoria, noticed Ton's swollen cheeks. "Did you fight again?" she said with faint disapproval.

"Ah, it was nothing. Just a little fun with the boys," Ton said.

"I wish you wouldn't, Ton, you know that."

It didn't take a genius to sense they had history.

"How'd the evening go for you ladies?" Ton asked.

"Oh, splendid, it was absolutely splendid," Victoria said, sitting upright and regal. *Now, here's a lady*, I thought to myself. "We sat in Box Nine in the Diamond section," she continued. "So nice of your Aunt Mamie to offer us her seats. And Emma Calvé was just divine."

Ton snuck Pat a smile, and I knew why. On our way to the Met they'd talked about how "divine" it was to have avoided the opera.

Now, at that time, I didn't know much about Emma Calvé, but, having lugged *The World* all over the streets of Manhattan the previous few weeks, I had noticed the headlines celebrating her role as Carmen. And now, looking back, I chuckle at the irony of Victoria saying that the role of Carmen had been played divinely. That's because, very soon, a ray of sunshine from the West would make Ton forget about "proper" Eastern ladies like Victoria.

As we rode along in the carriage, Victoria glanced down at me, then back at Ton. "Shouldn't the young lad be in bed?"

"Aw, Mac's all right. He worked my corner."

She lowered her voice. "Don't you think you could just give him a little money rather than keep him up so late?"

"Mac doesn't take handouts," Ton said. "He's earned his keep. He runs a good corner."

I felt awful tall, hearing that.

"But doesn't he have school in the morning?" She looked over at me. "Do you have school in the morning, little one?"

"Yes, ma'am," I lied.

Get to bed for *school?* Shoot, I'd already started thinking about trying to sell more evening editions later that night. I'd be up early in the morning, all right, but not for school. She was clueless. But she carried herself so captivatingly and had the type of beauty that could make you spellbound—which is why, when we reached my tenement house, I scampered out of that carriage wondering what it would take to get a woman like that someday.

A couple days later, Ton walked up to buy a paper from me on his way to Columbia.

"Did you save those quarters for your mother?" he asked.

"Yep, sure did."

"Good on you, old boy. There's a restaurant on Fifth Avenue and Twenty-sixth, Delmonico's. You know the place?"

"Of course," I said. It was the city's most talked-about restaurant, frequented by Manhattan's elite.

"Good. What do you say about taking your mom there this Friday?"

"Sounds good."

"Ask for a guy named Sam," Ton said. "Tell him that Secretary Fish recommended the place and that the secretary wanted you to ask if Sam's wife was feeling any better. He'll treat you well."

"Are you gonna keep me on as your second?" I asked. All weekend I'd worried over the bout he'd lost, in part because it was his first loss with me in his corner. "I'm awfully sorry you took that fall."

"Of course, Mac, you're my guy. But I gotta tell you, old boy, crew is starting up soon. I won't be fighting again until next fall, maybe winter. I talked to the fellows, though, and we need a boathouse manager for this upcoming season. You up for it?"

"I think so. How do you go about it?" I asked.

"It's not that bad, really. At the end of the week you'll need to come down to the boathouse and wash and wax the boats, and generally keep the house clean. It'll take a good part of the day, but it'll pay a dollar. Oh, and you'll need to come to our races to help with carrying the boats about and making sure everything is squared away. But you get paid for that, too. What do you say?"

"A dollar?"

"That's right."

"I'm in."

***

That Friday, early evening, having scrubbed up, I stepped into our tenement's main room, in which sat our stove, a little sitting area, and my bed. My mom was standing by the stove, probably thinking about what to put together for dinner.

"Listen Mom, I've got a surprise for you tonight," I told her. "I've been saving a part of my earnings, and I'm taking you to a real restaurant."

"What are you talking about, Rory Mac?" she asked, dubious.

"I'm serious. We're going. I've saved up for it."

"Don't be silly. We'll keep that money in savings," she said.

"No, Momma, I promised Ton. He told me I must take you."

She looked at me, and I could tell that she realized I needed to do this. That this was important.

"Well, where are we going then?" she asked.

"Delmonico's."

Her eyes widened. "Have you gone mad, young man?"

"No, I'm not mad. You must come. I promised."

When she smiled, I knew she was in. And once she was in, she was all in. She put on a dress that I hadn't seen since before Dad died, and on our walk to Delmonico's I could feel that she was excited and proud to have her son escorting her.

Still, upon making it to Delmonico's grand front entrance, we were hesitant to walk inside. I'd never eaten at a real restaurant and I reckoned my mom hadn't either, especially one like Delmonico's. It didn't help that once we mustered up the courage to walk through the doorway, the host met us with a cold stare. I don't think my raggedy, hand-me-down suit, which was a couple sizes too small, impressed him.

"Can I help you?" he asked, barely glancing at me.

"Can I talk to Sam?" I asked, catching him off guard. He looked at me a bit cockeyed, but, to my surprise, went to get Sam.

"Hello, can I help you?" Sam asked, walking up.

"My mom and I would like a table, sir. Secretary Fish recommended your place, and he requested that I ask you how your wife's doing. Is her health recovering?"

"Oh my, yes, I'm sorry. Yes, Lucy is doing much better, thank you. Right this way, please follow me."

It was kings and queens after that. We were led to a table covered with cream-white linen that went to the floor, and there were fresh flowers in an ornate vase set on the table. Our chairs were pulled out by two attendants. It was an absolute hoot the way they treated us. In *The World*, I'd read about the U.S. Presidents who had eaten at Delmonico's, and the business magnates and vaudeville stars who also ate there. Now it was our turn.

We didn't have enough money for the Lobster Newburg, but we did get to put our fine silver to use by sharing a turkey roast. And we each enjoyed a block of Neapolitan for dessert. Ah, the Neapolitan. It might seem like a regular thing to folks nowadays, but I can still taste it, and I can still see my mom beaming as I looked across the table. It was like we were sharing a secret dream from which nobody could wake us. I think that's what Ton wanted. The picture I have in my mind of my mom from that night is the type that helps you fall asleep at night when it won't come easy.

Chapter 4

Between selling papers, working fights, and taking care of the boathouse, time sailed. By the end of the crew season of 1895—about a year and a half since I'd first met Ton—I'd grown a good deal taller and at least a little wiser. I'd risen a bit in the newsboy ranks, as well, and a time or two had even been asked to dig up information in Hell's Kitchen for a reporter chasing a beat. I'd read *Rob Roy* at Ton's urging, and I'd even kissed a girl. Oh, and I got a little woozy from whiskey for the first time. It happened on the twenty-fourth of June, 1895, the same day that I watched Ton pull Columbia to an upset victory at Poughkeepsie and become the talk of the sporting nation.

At this time, the Cuban-led insurrection against Spanish rule in Cuba—a rebellion that would, little as we might've guessed then, pull Ton and me into war—was well underway, but it wasn't getting much attention in America. There had been plenty of death and destruction in Cuba, to be sure, but at that time, Spain's General Weyler, known as The Butcher, hadn't yet forced hundreds of thousands of Cubans into relocation camps. Americans, most of whom leaned isolationist when it came to getting involved in other countries' affairs, simply weren't focused on Cuba. Folks in Poughkeepsie were paying a lot more attention to the crew race there that day. In fact, it seemed like that's all that New Jersey and New York could talk about.

If you listened to the dopesmiths, Columbia didn't have much of a chance of winning, but I was betting otherwise. We'd traveled up the Hudson to Poughkeepsie the day before the race so that the guys could get a training session in. After the practice run, we cleaned the boats and packed up gear before taking quarters in Poughkeepsie's Nelson Inn. The next morning I woke up to a flood of sunlight. It looked to be a great day for a race—a soft northwest wind smoothed the Hudson's waters, the sky was clear blue, and the sun shone down in that kind of way that just picks you up. I got the sense that something big was going to happen.

After eating a good breakfast with the fellows and checking on our equipment in the boathouse, I watched as people filled the Hudson's banks in anticipation of the race. By early afternoon, thousands of people lined the river's banks, basking in the sun, reveling in a beautiful early summer day. As race time neared, the anticipation heightened and space became even tighter. A group of kids about my age, looking for a good spot to watch the race, took to climbing onto the roof of a nearby church, while across the river hundreds of folks piled on top of an observation train which had stopped on a rail line that hugged the Hudson at Krum Elbow, near the race's starting point. Sunshine continued to pour down, at least for now, highlighting the Hudson's dark blues. And, my goodness, the ladies. Whether sitting on train-tops or walking along riverside paths, they dazzled. Maybe I was at the right age to be floored by 'em, I don't know, but it seemed like every looker from New York City to Buffalo decided to come to Poughkeepsie that day.

Back then they dressed like ladies, too. I'm talking about lawn dresses and cambric parasols, straw hats, ribbons, and furbelows. I'm talking about style. One lady in particular stands out in my mind's eye to this day. As she walked, her blue dress flowed right along with the river, and her strawberry-blond hair glistened in the sun.

Sure, I was only fourteen years old, but as far as I could tell, this was the most beautiful woman in the world. She spun guys around as she walked past them, even the ones who tried to make it seem like they didn't notice her.

I'd made friends with the boathouse boys from Cornell and Penn, and all three of us agreed that it was a fine way to put in time, looking out at the crowd and watching the river, feeling the sun, the energy, the anticipation. Little did we know a storm was a-brewing.

About an hour or two from start time the first signs of the storm appeared in the form of a powerful, whipping wind. Clouds and thunder soon rolled in, and flashes of lightning intermittently ripped through the sky. Then heavy rain began. Most of the spectators had scurried for cover by then, but a bunch of students from Columbia, perched on one of the train cars, stayed through the downpour, singing and laughing while they got soaked. I'd taken partial cover under a big oak tree.

In the middle of the deluge, I watched the legendary John Jacob Astor IV—the same Astor scion that would die in 1912 aboard the *Titanic*—arrive by way of an "electric launch" motorboat, which I'd never seen before. The boat motored right upriver through the rain before pulling onto a gentle part of the riverbank, across from where I stood. Mr. Astor and his crew took cover till the rain stopped. Then they found a spot on top of one of the train cars to watch the race.

Sitting up on the trains gave a great view of things, but I didn't plan on watching from there. The day prior, for a few copper heads, I'd gotten a local kid to let me borrow his bicycle during the race, the idea being that I could ride it on the walking path along the river, up off the bank a bit, and stay in line with the sculls as they raced. The main challenge would be finagling my way through the people sitting or otherwise milling about in the grass.

When the rain finally let up, I delivered word to the fellows in the boathouse that it was time to race. They immediately took on an air of resolve. Sizing them up, I reckoned they'd win, that the half-dollar I'd put on them before leaving the city would indeed reap something. Under a thick haze, I helped Ton and the guys carry their boat down to the river. They moved into starting position alongside the Cornell and Penn teams. Twenty-one minutes was all that separated one of these squads from victory and celebratory coverage in the nation's newspapers.

The sound of the starter gun ripped through the air, and all three teams came out hard. During the first mile Cornell and Penn kept pace with Ton's crew, but early into mile two Columbia edged ahead, even as wind-against-tide caused the rowers to splash more than usual. It was this rough stretch of water that highlighted the advantage of Ton's vaunted strength. I'm not overstating matters when I tell you that Ton literally pulled Columbia ahead. The papers I sold the next day recognized as much, declaring him the "giant of Columbia's Varsity." By the end of mile two, Columbia held a clear, yet still modest, edge.

To stay in line with the boats for the gut-wrenching last mile, I had to weave my bicycle around people. I would switch from looking to my side to keep an eye on the boats, to looking ahead so that I didn't run anyone over, then back again.

Columbia slowly but steadily built upon its lead.

Ton and his mates were pulling with all their might, yet in rhythm and with poise. They won by five lengths. My arms went up in the air in celebration just like Ton's, as did the arms of thousands of rain-soaked Columbia fans sitting on the train cars and the Hudson's banks.

My word, did that victory set off a celebration! Poughkeepsie was usually a quiet town, the kind of place that hadn't moved from sulfur to parlor matches, but on this night it gave New Orleans a run. Soon after Columbia's victory, the Blue and White's supporters had seized control of the town's main streets. Columbia's coach, Walter B. Peet, and Ton and the rest of the boys, me included, were paraded through town to rousing cheers. Joe Lawrence, who had rowed for Columbia in the mid-1880s, drummed up a brass band that played riffs on college airs and belted out popular fare from Sousa and the like. Fans sang along and danced and cheered.

By and by, the main patch of revelers and Joe Lawrence's band set up a base of celebratory operations out in front of the Nelson House Inn, making it the party's epicenter for the rest of the night. The other boathouse boys and I found some Old Overholt on the sly, which we managed to pour into a few innocent-looking mugs. We tried to stay inconspicuous as we milled about looking at the beautiful ladies.

The young lady I'd noticed earlier, with the blue dress, strawberry-blonde hair, and greenish-blue eyes, caught my attention again. She was walking in our direction.

"She's a beaut," I said to the other boathouse boys as she approached.

"Yeah, she's something," Bobby from Penn said.

And then all of a sudden something amazing happened. She smiled at me. My heart thumped; my throat went dry.

"Did you see that?" I asked.

"I think she might've smiled at you," Charlie, the Cornell boy, said. "You should talk to her when she comes back around."

"Are you crazy? What am I going to say?"

"Tell her you're tired from the race you just won. She won't know any different."

"I can't lie to her. Did you see her? She's not the type of woman you lie to."

"Then tell her you're fourteen and you had to sneak Overholt into that cup."

We laughed at that. But then I started sweating and my skin turned white. It happened that fast. I swallowed hard as beads of sweat came streaming down my forehead. For a moment I thought I was dying. Then I ran over to a nearby patch of grass and threw up. The other boathouse boys had come over and stared at me wide-eyed. "You all right?" one of them asked.

"Yeah," I said, before throwing up again. Apparently, I wasn't ready for Overholt.

I pulled myself together, and we made our way back over to the crowd out in front of the Nelson Inn. Pretty soon we were watching Ton and his crewmates and several of the older alums, backed by the band, singing the Columbia fight song. Next, it was Sousa's "The Band Played On!" to which Ton and his buddies waltzed with ladies in the street. For the next number, Ton partnered with the strawberry blond in the blue dress. *That's a lucky man*, I thought.

By midnight, the streets had largely cleared out. Most of the ladies had turned in, while most of the fellows had found their way to nearby pubs. Ton, his racing buddies, and the other boathouse boys and me ended up in a game parlor in the basement of the Nelson House Inn. The parlor had a Berliner with a George Johnson tune playing, three tables for card games, a roulette wheel off in one corner, and a small side table, at which Charlie and Bobby and I, our heads starting to clear a bit, took up our own game of blackjack. Ton took a seat at one of the main poker tables.

Not long after we arrived, a rowdy group of men rambled down the stairs that led into the parlor. It appeared right-quick that these fellows had spent too much time at the ale house across the way. They were talking too loud and acting bellicose. One of them seemed particularly fiery—a guy named Wiley, who was a loud-mouth from the get-go. I found out later that he'd come into the parlor hot on account of his girl having danced with the collegians on Market Street. Anyway, Wiley and another one of the fellows in this rowdy group sat down and started playing poker, not at Ton's table, though.

They remained loud and aggressive while they played cards. They sent up roars of approval, for instance, when a hand went their way, which everyone else found rather annoying, especially since it seemed like the cards were breaking their way. They made light of the college "boys," too. The longer they played, the tenser the place got.

An hour or so after the rowdies had arrived, at about 1:30 in the morning, the money at two of the poker tables got squared away, and it looked like matters were about to wrap up at the third. Ton, thinking his evening was finished, stood up from his table and headed toward the stairs. On his way, he happened by the last table—the one at which Wiley was playing. As he was walking past he paused. Instead of continuing on, he stood, unassumingly enough, behind one the poker players, the Cornell captain he had whipped on the Hudson several hours prior.

Soon, this Cornell captain, thinking perhaps he could score a big win before turning in, raised an already sizable pot. In turn, Wiley pulled out two hundred dollars and declared, "I'll cover that, and I'll put another hundred on top of it." This was the night's biggest hand.

The man in red seemed to hedge, but a teammate sitting next to him urged him on. I was standing just behind them, not far from Ton, and I could overhear the teammate tell his captain, "I'll help cover. He's bluffing. Let's take him."

"I'm in and then some," Wiley's target concluded, producing the requisite sum, plus a hundred more.

I'd never seen anywhere near that much scrap in one place at one time.

"Ah, the gentleman wants to risk daddy's money. I see what's going on here. But you can't push me out. I'll not only see it, I'll venture two hundred more," Wiley said, smacking down the money. "What's it gonna be, then?"

The room was silent for several moments as eyes moved back and forth from Wiley to the Cornell captain. Ultimately, there wasn't much left to do except cover and let the cards fall where they may. This is what the man from Ithaca did, with the help of his teammate, who slipped him a couple hundred bucks. Having put the money down, the Cornell captain took a long look at Wiley and then placed three kings and two eights on the table. The crowd gasped. He'd come strong with a full house.

But then Wiley stood up, leaned over the table, and laid down four aces. Grabbing the loot, he said, "Four aces, you damn big money dude!"

As Wiley pulled the money away, a hand came down hard upon his arm, pinning his wrist to the table. I turned to look who'd done it and saw Ton. And then, as quickly as he'd brought his hand down upon Wiley's wrist, Ton reached up Wiley's sleeve and pulled out three cards.

"Best let go of that money," Ton said plainly.

All hell broke loose then. The Ithacans grabbed for their money, while Wiley's men came in on Ton. Everyone started throwing punches. Shoot, even me and the other boathouse boys jumped on the back of one of Wiley's ruffians. We tore that gambling den up good. The roulette wheel ended up on the ground; chairs were thrown about; a table caved in when men landed on it. We had the numbers advantage, though, and soon enough we pushed Wiley and his crew out of the Nelson House and back onto Market Street. Wiley, in fact, who, between the ale and the walloping Ton had given him, had become quite groggy, was thrown onto the street—Ton held him by the shoulders and Pat by the ankles as they chucked him.

As Ton righted himself, a few policemen dashed onto the scene. One of them came up quickly and unexpectedly on Ton's side. Unaware that it was a copper, Ton swung around quick as a whip, leading with his right hand, which landed square on the policeman's jaw, sending him down. Realizing what he'd done, Ton immediately tried to apologize, but the policemen could only take so much. They took him to the Poughkeepsie pen along with a few of the other brawlers.

Chapter 5

Before he was hauled off by the police, Ton told me not to worry and asked that I let his parents know in the morning that he'd run into a little jam but was fine.

"Where do your parents live?" I asked.

"Fifty-three Irving Place," he said, before being hauled off.

Several hours later, having picked up a bundle of *The World* with front-page coverage of the race, I worked my way to Kips Bay, selling copies as I clipped along. Upon reaching the Fish residence—an impressive brick townhouse, but not one of those wildly extravagant ones—I knocked on the door. A young lady's maid answered with a smile, but once she had a chance to really look me over, her smile shifted to a look of uncertainty. I'd slept only about an hour, and I realized I probably looked pretty ragged.

"Is Mr. Fish in?" I asked.

"Yes, he is. Is he expecting you?"

"I don't think so."

"Can you tell me what you need him for?"

"No, ma'am."

"Well, I'm not sure…"

"I work for *The World*," I said, "I have important information. He'll want to hear it. Trust me."

Still skeptical, she led me into the anteroom before going to get Mr. Fish. Ton's dog, Chuck Jr., appeared. He smelled me and nuzzled up to me, which made me feel better. Ton had told me about Chuck Jr., that he was a good dog, like Charlie, the little Skye terrier that Ton had grown up with. And that was saying something. He'd been only twelve when Charlie died, and Ton couldn't eat or sleep for two days afterward.

Within a minute or so Mr. Fish appeared.

"Nicholas Fish," he said, outstretching his hand. "Whom do I have the pleasure of meeting?"

"Rory MacGregor, sir."

"Nice to meet you, Rory. How can I help you?"

"Um, uh, sir, I was…well, uh, Ton asked me to let you know that he's…well, he's in a bit of a fix up in Poughkeepsie."

He looked at me sort of sideways.

"What kind of a fix?" he asked.

"You see, sir, I'm the boathouse manager for Columbia, and, well, you know they won the race last evening, right?"

"Yes, I know. I was there, young man. What do you mean by a 'fix'?"

"Well, sir, he had a bit of a run-in with some fellows, some rowdy guys, and, well, as far as I can tell, he's in the pen up there in Poughkeepsie."

Mr. Fish rolled his eyes a bit, which made me think he wasn't terribly surprised.

"It wasn't his fault, really," I said. "You should've seen it. He stopped this sharp from cheating a fellow from Cornell out of a mighty stack. And then, once the brawl started—"

"How old are you?" Mr. Fish interrupted.

"I'm fourteen, sir."

He reached for his wallet and said, "Well, thank you for your trouble, lad. I'll take care of it from here." Then he tried to hand me a few bills.

"No, thank you, sir," I said, pulling away. "Coming here wasn't work, sir."

"All right, then," he said matter-of-factly. "Thank

you for letting me know."

***

From there I worked my way to the entrance of Columbia, hawking along the way. Late in the morning a lull came, giving me a chance to read the paper more fully. I was happy to see that *The World* hadn't mentioned Ton's arrest. And yet it gave darn near four full pages of ink to the race, describing each boat, the crowd, the weather, the famous attendees, and Ton's vaunted strength. It was something.

Alongside the front-page article on the race, I noticed a story about Cuba. It was titled "To Dynamite Havana," and in it a Cuban insurgent talked about his desire to make a careful study of explosives while he was in America, in the hopes of one day blowing Spanish ships out of the sea. "We will begin with Havana and give the Spanish a few lessons…We want something effective; something that will let daylight and civilization into Spanish barbarism," he said. As I say, little did I know that Ton and I would be in Cuba in a few short years.

A couple days removed from the Poughkeepsie pen, Ton stopped by my favorite corner to pick up a paper. He thanked me for getting word to his father and mentioned that Columbia was giving him a hard time for getting thrown in the pen, while the Nelson Inn had raised hay over its gambling parlor getting torn up—ironic, seeing as the gambling was illegal to begin with. But Mr. Fish didn't want a drawn-out row, so he'd sent a few thousand dollars upriver to smooth things over.

Apparently, Columbia was talking about suspending Ton, though, and making him finish classes in the fall. That scenario didn't seem likely to me. Ton hadn't even walked with his graduating class several weeks earlier, even though he could have, and for some time now he hadn't exactly paid much attention to his studies. He had a particular distaste for his Greek and Latin assignments—he considered them outdated—and he had a kind of aversion to graduating, like it was an overly elitist thing to do. He'd made it clear to his buddies that he didn't need a diploma to be made whole, which is why they liked to rib him for being dangerously close to earning one. "I want to be informed, not academic," he told me a time or two.

He got his wish later that summer when Columbia told him he'd have to return to school for the fall semester to complete unfinished coursework. This didn't happen. For months, Ton's mind had been turning westward and nothing, certainly not school, was going to keep him from heading there. He figured, *to hell with it; I've learned what I wanted. They can keep the degree.* His parents wanted him to stay and finish, but I bet they knew it wasn't happening.

* * *

Ton finally cut the cord on the elite life at perhaps the biggest social event of the year for the elite set: Gertrude Vanderbilt's debutante ball in Newport, Rhode Island. As I say, the lifestyles of the elites in the realm within which the Fishes ran were legendary. I'm talking about people with sprawling mansions along Bellevue Avenue and Ocean Drive for Newport's famed summer season; people who commissioned fake trees replete with golden leaves, who bought jewels like others bought chocolate squares.

The Vanderbilts wanted to introduce their daughter in a way that would stand out even within this realm, and they did. The multi-course dinner ball took place at their summer estate, which had a thirty-foot-high wrought iron entryway, with intricate, golden rocailles and fleurs-de-lis. Its lawns, impeccably manicured, were packed with elms and maples. The home itself, *The Breakers*, was made of Indiana limestone and covered 65,000 square feet. Its great hall, modeled on Roman atriums, had a 45-foot-high ceiling. There were rooms with walls of cream-colored Caen stone and floors of Italian and African marble. More than 30 full-time servants attended to the place, and extra help was hired to plan for the signature ball.

A few years later, as we lay in camp in San Antonio, Ton told me about how midway through the evening portion of the ball, he walked into the Breakers' main library and gazed at a massive limestone chimneypiece upon which was an inscription that read: "Little do I care for riches, and do not miss them, since only cleverness prevails in the end." It struck him as richly ironic to read that quote in that house, at that ball, at that time in his life.

So much seemed to exist under a superficial glaze to him. His supposed relationship with Victoria lacked any real depth. He had no passion for the job offers he had in the banking world. He could imagine the life he'd have if he stayed. It was the kind of life that he knew ladies like Victoria desperately wanted: a home base in Manhattan, trips to Europe, summers in Newport, immaculate balls, appearances at the opera, social visits, carriage rides, leisure…and men in whitetails, foxhunting and playing polo, working for a bank, joining social clubs, owning fine art.

He didn't want that. He wanted out. In fact, this feeling seized him so strongly that he nearly busted out of his white tie and tailcoat right there, nearly broke out of the place like a wild man. Instead, he put in action a plan to head West.

Chapter 6

If you only read Pulitzer's *The World*, you'd have thought that Ton was so eager to make it on his own out West, to break with the privileges that came with the class into which he was born, that he'd given up a prime railroad berth offered by his uncle to get there, and that he arrived in Salt Lake City without any advantages. In truth, he left Manhattan with letters from his uncle—the president of the Illinois Central Railroad—along with several trunks of clothes and flush with cash. Still, he didn't expect an easy route. He planned on working. And, in the ensuing months, he would toil in just about every capacity a railroad man could: in the freight house, the local shops, and as a brakeman on the main line.

Initially, Ton stayed in Salt Lake only one night, long enough to secure a room, unpack his things, and meet up with a buddy named Walters, a former classmate from Columbia. Before Ton would settle in Utah, the two had planned a trip to Globe, Arizona, to visit a mine Ton had invested in.

The mine was owned by a fellow named Adolph Lewishon, a wealthy businessman Ton had met months earlier in Manhattan at a family dinner party. Mr. Lewishon had told Ton about a mining firm that he and his brothers had recently purchased in Arizona.

"The future is in electricity, and you need copper if you want electricity," Mr. Lewishon had declared.

The two hit it off so well that by night's end, Mr. Lewishon had offered Ton a job, but Ton had his eye on rail work. Ton did mention, though, that he had some cash available through a family trust, and that he was interested in investing in the mine. Mr. Lewishon heard this type of talk at dinner parties all the time, but few people were willing to actually risk money in a desolate Western state that still faced problems with Apaches—especially given that a couple of years prior, the Sherman Silver Purchase Act had been repealed, walloping Arizona's mining business. Yet he sensed that Ton was different, and he figured it couldn't hurt to have a family like the Fishes connected to his mine. So he followed up with him. To Ton, the idea of investing in the future in a wild and woolly state like Arizona was appealing. Plus, it gave him an excuse to visit the place.

Getting to Lewishon's Arizona mine presented some major challenges, seeing as some seven hundred miles separated it from Salt Lake City—much of that mileage desolate and unreachable by rail. Undeterred, Ton and Walters set out feeling energized and adventurous. They spent several full days traveling by horseback. Most of the time they camped out in the wild, although a time or two they found a local saloon at which they could oil up and, for a dollar or two, each rent a bunk for the night. Here and there, to break the monotony of traveling all day, they'd visit a reservation—only the ones known to be safe—or go hunting. All in all, it wasn't easy living, but Ton loved it. And he came away from Mr. Lewishon's mine as an investor.

It would prove a smart bet.

Upon returning to Utah, Ton went to work for a standard-gauge offshoot of a family of rail lines known as the Rio Grande. The Rio Grande's tracks crossed much of the West, passing through epic mountains along the way. These passes were engineering marvels, and they made the firm known the world over. The company's ability to cut through mountains, in fact, had prompted the tagline:

"Through the Rockies, Not Around Them," and it had inspired the stylized "Rio Grande" speed-lettering that the firm plastered on its rail cars. By the time Ton started working there, the Rio Grande had one of the nation's most recognizable logos.

The lines that Ton worked connected Utah with Colorado and were used mainly to bring mineral reserves to Salt Lake City. From there, the minerals would get shipped to the rest of the country. The work was difficult and dangerous, but, as I say, Ton didn't mind most of it. He thought it put hair on his chest.

He started out in the local freight depot before getting transferred to Provo Canyon to carry chain for surveyors. He liked the view of the Timpanogos mountain range in Provo, but he didn't like carrying chain, nor did he aspire to become a surveyor. So at his first chance, he transferred back to Salt Lake to work in the brake shop and on general line repair, which suited him fine. In Salt Lake, there were more Easterners to hit up watering holes with, anyhow.

It wasn't long after his transfer back to Salt Lake that Ton met Jane Witherspoon. He'd been sent to repair a section of line several miles outside of town, where the tracks seemed to stretch endlessly, and head-high purple sage and the occasional aspen bordered the line. Focused on pounding a large nail into a railroad tie, he didn't notice Jane as she approached on horseback.

"Hello there, sir," she called out, as she guided her horse through a break in the sage.

Startled a bit, Ton turned and looked up. Framed by a blue sky and illuminated by a bright sun, sat a strikingly beautiful woman upon a horse. Her beauty knocked him off balance for a moment. He suddenly remembered that he'd taken off his cotton-bib on account of the heat, and this made him self-conscious. She seemed unaffected. Gathering himself, Ton side-stepped over to his horse to put his shirt back on, then tipped his Stetson and said, "Well, hello there, Miss."

"I was wondering, sir," Jane said, "if you've seen or heard any stray cattle nearby."

"No need to call me sir, Miss," Ton said, having slid his shirt back on. He reached up to shake her hand. "The name's Ton. Ton Fish."

When their hands touched, a charge surged through his body. He looked down to try to play it off. Sure, the setting worked to Jane Witherspoon's advantage: sitting upon a fine horse with Utah's majestic Oquirrh Mountains strengthening the horizon, purple sage gently swaying in the near background, the sun shining down behind her. But truth be told, just about every setting worked for Jane Witherspoon, what with her sun-kissed cheeks, blue-green, self-assured eyes, warm smile, and long blond hair.

"I'm Jane Witherspoon," she said. "Nice to meet you."

"Likewise." Ton couldn't help but be distracted now by Jane's long legs—her cowboy boots darn near reached the ground.

Jane looked up and down the railroad line. "Well, Ton Fish, have you seen any cattle?" she asked again.

"Oh, yeah. I mean, no, I haven't," Ton said.

"All right, then, Mr. Fish. Take care, now." With that, Jane turned her horse to head back through the sage.

"Will do, Miss Jane Witherspoon."

A plume of dust rose up as her horse trotted away and, just like that, she was gone.

For the rest of the day, Ton couldn't get her out of his mind. He knew that he had to see her again, and soon. He started plotting a way to do just that.

***

He began by gathering information through Johnnie Reid, a young man he'd befriended. About Ton's age, Johnnie had lived in Salt Lake most of his life, had graduated from Brigham Young, and worked for a firm that did business with the Rio Grande. That weekend, then, while they threw mule shoes, Ton said, "I met this lady the other day while I was out working on the line. Her name's Jane Witherspoon. You ever heard of her?"

Johnnie smiled, clearly amused. "Have I ever heard of Jane Witherspoon?"

"Yes. What's so funny?"

"She's only Salt Lake's most coveted bachelorette."

"Is that right?"

"Well, look at her, I mean, she's gorgeous—plus, she's smart, independent, and the daughter of a mega-rancher who happens to be a church elder. So, yes, I've heard of her."

"Alright, I get it," Ton said, smiling as he threw a mule shoe.

"She lives a few miles outside of town on the Witherspoon Ranch," Johnnie explained. "Attends the occasional picnic but doesn't socialize too much. Mainly, she works hard on the ranch. And apparently she reads voraciously. Some say she reads too much—she catches a little flack for her progressive ways. Progressive for out here, that is."

"That so?"

"She doesn't kowtow, let's put it that way. She takes classes, too, at the University of Utah, which makes some fellows a little uncomfortable. She studies under Maude May Babcock, the playwright and suffragist, and acts in her plays occasionally."

"She sounds fine to me," said Ton.

"Yeah, well, plenty of men would agree, but it's like she's hard to get to. And she's Mormon, Ton. You know that, right?"

Ton shrugged, undeterred.

Chapter 7

A few days later Ton strode up to the desk of Mrs. Smith, a receptionist at the University of Utah's School of Elocution and Physical Culture. He tipped his hat and said, "Hello, ma'am."

"Hello. How can I help you?"

"My name's Ton Fish and, uh, I was wondering if I could sit in on one of Miss Babcock's classes." He swallowed hard, his throat a little dry.

She looked at him with a hint of a smile. "You'd like to sit in on the drama class starting in five minutes?"

"That's right, if you don't mind?"

"Well, I'd say this is pretty original." She paused. "I'll ask. She might very well allow it."

A short time later, the receptionist returned. "You can attend," she said, smiling.

"Thank you, Mrs. Smith," Ton said, starting down the hallway. "I'm mighty grateful."

Before he got more than a few steps, Mrs. Smith said: "Hey there, Mr. Ton Fish."

"Yes?" He turned to look back.

"You read Shakespeare much?"

"On occasion."

"You know she's like Rosaline, right?" she asked, smiling.

Ton hesitated a moment then smiled back. "I know not of what or whom you speak, Mrs. Smith."

Ton introduced himself to Miss Babcock and grabbed a seat in the back. A few minutes later, Jane walked in. On her way to a seat near the front, she glanced upward. Her eyes happened to meet Ton's, and she paused a moment and smiled ever so slightly, lifting him right up.

It was time for class to start and once underway, Ton quickly realized that Miss Babcock's reputation as a task-master was warranted. Small groups of students would come up to the front to present short scenes, which she'd critique. "Say it like you mean it," she'd direct. "Stand straight, like a man." "Pick your head up." "Have more passion."

Near the end of class Miss Babcock looked at Ton and said, "Ton, as our guest, would you like to give it a try?"

"Um, no, thanks, Miss. I'm all right."

"Oh, I'm sorry, I wasn't really asking. I guess I should've said, 'Sir, please come to the front,'" she responded.

Without much choice in the matter, Ton did as he was told.

"Do you know of *A Midsummer Night's Dream*?" she asked.

"A little bit."

"Well, here's a sheet if you need any help with the lines. Jane, why don't you play Thisbe for us?" Miss Babcock asked.

Jane, looking a little flustered, said, "Sure." She got up and stood a few feet across from Ton. Meanwhile, Miss Babcock rolled over a thin prop wall that she positioned between Ton and Jane as a barrier. They couldn't see each other, but they were close enough to touch.

"All right, then," Miss Babcock said. "Begin."

Speaking through the thin wall, Jane started: "My love! Thou art my love, I think."

Ton, his knees a little wobbly, responded: "Think what thou wilt, I am thy lover's grace; And, like Limander, am I trusty still."

Caught up in the text, they traded lines:
And I like Helen, till the Fates me kill.
   Not Shafalus to Procrus was so true.
As Shafalus to Procrus, I to you.
O! kiss me through the hole of this vile wall!
I kiss the wall's hole, not your lips at all.
Wilt thou at Ninny's tomb meet me straightway?
'Tide life, 'tide death, I come without delay.

After Jane's final line, Ton slid the cardboard prop to the side and met her gaze with his own, his heart thumping.

"That was actually pretty good," Miss Babcock said. "I could feel it. Ton, you went a little fast. But all in all, good job."

Ton and Jane stepped offstage, both self-conscious, hesitant to look the other in the eye.

Outside after class, Ton walked alongside Jane.

"So, you're thinking about studying acting under Miss Babcock?" she asked coyly, walking toward her hitched horse.

"Kicking it around," Ton hedged. "Based on today, I might very well have a future."

"With the stage?"

"I don't know. What do you think? Is there a future?"

"I'm not sure," Jane parried as she mounted her horse and reached for the reins. "It's not easy."

"I suppose," Ton said. "Can I see you again?"

Jane looked at him. "I don't know."

"Well, I'd like to take you to a proper dinner."

"Like Miss Babcock said, I think you might be going a little fast."

"Well, how about this; for the next few days I'm

working along the same portion of track where you saw me the other day—amid the sage, a few leagues without the town, as they say. Perhaps, if you're out that way looking for cattle again, you can take a break for lunch?"

"Perhaps," she said. Then she gently urged her horse forward and started toward the mountains again.

***

By the third morning after seeing Jane in Miss Babcock's class, Ton's spirits dropped. He had not seen Jane since, and his head was aching on account of having drunk too much the night before. Dealing with the blazing sun and pounding nails into railroad tie after tie didn't help the headache either.

He decided to take matters into his own hands. He'd brought a sheet of paper and some string with him to work. Now, with lunch approaching, he hopped on his horse and rode a mile or so toward the Witherspoon Ranch. As he approached, he saw Jane working out in a big field among a group of cattle, just as he'd hoped. A couple of other ranchers were further off a ways, working cattle, too.

Ton was still a good stretch away from Jane, far enough not to be recognized but close enough to be noticed. He didn't wave. He simply rode up toward a calf that had broken away from the group and used his string to tie a sheet of paper to its ear. Then, he turned his horse around and rode back to the stretch of rail he was working on.

Intrigued, Jane rode over to the stray calf, dismounted, and walked slowly up to it. She saw on the sheet of paper the word LUNCH, with an arrow pointing in Ton's direction. She smiled and went back to work; she'd have to wait a few minutes to avoid provoking suspicion. But after letting a short interval pass, she peeled off.

Ton took a swig of Coca-Cola from his thermos, hoping it'd clear his head. As he grabbed his sandwich, he thought he heard something. It was faint, but it sounded like the hooves he'd been waiting to hear for three days. Through a break in the sage up ahead, he saw Jane come into view, sun shining down all around. Elated, he waved her over.

"Glad you could make it," he said as she dismounted. "You hungry?"

"Thank you, I am. I heard there was lunch out this way."

"You heard right. I've got a sandwich here for you."

"Very good."

She accepted a cup of water from him, then took a seat on a railroad tie. Ton sat down next to her.

She scanned the horizon to the Oquirrh Mountains, then gazed up and down the tracks. "How's your work coming along?"

"Fine. Mostly poundin' in pins and diggin' up old ties today."

"Sandwich is good," she said, savoring a bite. "Thank you."

"You're welcome. You ever have a Fig Newton?"

"Never had one before."

"Here you go. Straight from the New York Biscuit Company—a little piece of home."

"So I hear."

"Oh yeah, you know I'm from New York?"

"I do."

"And what else might you have heard about me?"

"What haven't I? People around town tend to talk."

"That right?"

"Let's see if I have it right: part of the illustrious Fish family, captain of Columbia's eight, member of St. Anthony Hall and the Union League, rumors of boxing—"

"Interesting."

"There's more."

"Oh yeah?"

"Might not have finished his studies on account of an arrest. Might be spoken for. Might be a little rowdy."

He hadn't expected her frankness, but he liked it.

"Mmm. Well, some of that's true; let me clear it up a little for you. As for school, I didn't care too much for Greek and Latin, I'll admit that. As for an arrest, I suppose you're referring to Poughkeepsie?"

"There's been more than one?"

"All I can tell you is that the bully-sharp I tangled with in Poughkeepsie had it coming. He was a cheat, plain and simple."

"Is that so?"

"That's so. Now, as for being spoken for, I'm not," Ton said, looking her in the eyes. She smiled a little. Their connection was undeniable. "You know," he went on, "I've heard a little about you."

"Really?" she said, intrigued.

"Daughter of a wealthy, ranch-owning church elder; a little feisty; progressive-minded but at the same time conservative, at least when it comes to courting, which she is not known to participate in, basically at all."

"Interesting."

"Oh, and I've been told more than once that she's Mormon."

"Well, that's true."

"How Mormon?"

"What does that mean? How Protestant are you?"

"That's a good question," Ton said. "Enough to keep an open mind."

She smiled.

They ate for a bit in silence, looking down the line, at the purple sage, and the mountains beyond, until Ton asked, "So what's Jane Witherspoon's favorite author of all time?"

"Mmm…Charlotte Brontë."

"I can see that," Ton said.

"Your turn."

"Hawthorne. I like Twain too, on account of *Roughing It*, which is hilarious. And, of course, *Huckleberry Finn*."

"I'll give you Hawthorne," Jane said. "But in these parts you might want to keep your appreciation for *Roughing It* to yourself."

"I guess you're right. I'm sorry, I wasn't thinking, I—"

"Because you know us Mormon women, we're so ugly and all."

"I think Twain was just satirizing polygamy, which you're not for, right?"

"Of course not. Still, his take on Mormons reads like chloroform in print."

"I understand." Hoping to change the subject, Ton stood up. "Miss Witherspoon, have you ever changed out a railroad tie?"

"No. Can't say that I have."

"Let's give it a go."

He grabbed his pick-shovel and dug out an old rail tie that he'd started in on before lunch. He yanked the old tie out and replaced it with a new one.

"Now we've just got to pound these pins into this

new tie," he said, as he picked up a large hammer and handed it to her. He bent down to hold the spike in place.

"Don't hit my hand," Ton half-joked, looking up at her.

"Are you serious?" Jane asked, smiling. "I've never done this."

"Sure. Give it a go."

She raised the hammer, which was pretty heavy, and brought it down slowly, giving the spike a tap.

"Oh come on Miss Witherspoon, hit it," Ton said.

"All right," she said, reaching back before bringing the hammer down again. This time the hammer hit only the top edge of the pin before sliding off the side of it, right onto a few of Ton's fingers as he pulled them away.

"Oooohhhh, my!" Ton hollered, popping upright and hopping about, shaking his hand. He didn't know whether to scream or laugh.

Jane was horrified. "I'm so sorry. Are you all right?"

"Yeah, yeah, I'm fine," Ton said, walking in a circle and holding his fingers. "Oooo-eee. Let's try that again."

"No way."

"We've got to," Ton said, getting back into position. "We can't end with that."

Ton reset the spike. This time Jane hit it square. After a few more cracks the spike went in clean. "Once you get it going, it's not too hard," Jane said.

"Yeah, once you break through."

She looked down the track and over at her horse. The time had passed quickly.

"I should get going now," she said. "One of the ranch hands might get a little worried and come looking for me."

"I'd like to see you again," Ton said.

Jane smiled, but then she looked off in the direction of the ranch and sighed. Turning back to Ton, she said, "It's not that easy, you know?"

"Why not?"

They were silent for a little bit. Then Jane spoke again. "Give me a little time. I know where to find you. All right?"

Ton nodded.

Before mounting her horse, Jane leaned in and kissed him on the cheek. Ton's heart was still thumping as he listened to the hoofbeats trail away.

A few minutes later, back to work, he was startled by the sound of a horse. Ton looked up from the line as a dark-dressed man astride a horse appeared through the sage. It was Ben, a ranch hand at the Witherspoon Ranch, and he didn't look happy. He spat to the side as he drew the horse to a stop.

"Can I help you?" Ton asked.

"I tracked her, and I know what you all are up to," the man said. "I've got a message for you from the old man: Stay away from her before this gets ugly." Then, he tipped his cap and left.

Chapter 8

Within hours of their lunch together, murmurings about Jane Witherspoon and Ton Fish had worked their way through the Wasatch Valley. I don't think either of them realized how quickly they'd feel the pressure, or how tough it'd be for them, coming from different backgrounds, to see things through.

Ton had seen the way Jane looked at him when she asked him to give her time. So he tried to turn his focus to his work.

Soon he was transferred to the brake shop, where he learned how to repair pressure gauges and the like. He found the work interesting, and he liked that it was physically demanding, which made not seeing Jane easier. A hard week of labor, though, hadn't kept him from wondering when they'd meet again.

Two weeks passed with no new developments. By day, Ton continued working in the brake shop; at night, he often met up with his Eastern buddies at the Cannon Ball or some other establishment, where he surely drank more than he should've, trying, at least in part, to forget about Jane for a bit. He and his buddies would talk about all manner of things—the upcoming election between McKinley and Bryan, the New York Giants' diamond woes, whether U.S. money should be backed by gold or silver or both—but Jane was still never far from Ton's mind.

About to leave work one day, still feeling aimless, Ton got word that there was mail waiting on him at the Rio Grande's headquarters downtown. On his way home, he stopped in the main office to pick up the unaddressed letter. He opened it quickly.

Dear Ton,

How peculiar it is to find ourselves in this fix, the same type of romantic circumstance that our literary idols have written about over the ages. But somehow things seem harder to figure out in real life than in books. I hope you understand.

I would like to talk again in person. Perhaps you could meet me at the top of Arsenal Hill, near the old munitions depot, at midnight this Tuesday. There we can find the quiet we need to discuss matters further.

Sincerely,
Miss Jane Witherspoon

The letter sent a jolt through Ton. *There's hope*, he thought.

***

Ton arrived at the top of Arsenal Hill first, taking cover behind a clump of trees.

As Jane approached, he stepped out into the open and quietly called out.

"I'm sorry we have to meet this way," she said, visibly nervous. "I just had to talk to you."

"Of course. I understand."

She reached out and took him by the arm, leading him to the side of the depot, where a tree gave them cover before they sat down.

"Listen, Jane," Ton said. "I want you to know that my feelings for you are strong. I've never felt like this before."

"I know. I feel it too." Jane looked away. But when Ton took her by the hand, she turned back to him.

"Listen," he said. "We can leave here. Let's just go."

Jane took a deep breath and sighed. "I don't think it's that easy."

"Why not?"

"It's just that…I must respect my family. Maybe if we give it time, maybe our differences could be better understood. I mean…are you sure you're ready to just up and run off, settle down, and get married?"

"Well, under normal conditions, I suppose we should get to know each other." Ton smiled. "But these aren't normal conditions."

Ton was a romantic, she realized. She believed Ton meant what he said, but she could tell that he hadn't really thought it all through. She wondered if the passion Ton felt now would last. And she was only eighteen years old. As strong as her feelings were, she wasn't yet ready to make a clean break from her father, and from her life, from her people. Still, she wanted Ton.

Stalling, Jane looked out over Arsenal Hill, down to Salt Lake City below and the mountains beyond. It would've felt peaceful and quiet up there if her mind wasn't reeling. *It shouldn't be this hard. It really shouldn't.*

"From up here, everything looks so beautiful," she said. Ton nodded.

Close to his side now, Jane took his hand in hers, and soon they lay on their backs, her head resting on Ton's shoulder. For a long time neither spoke. They just gazed at the stars. After a time, Ton propped himself up on his elbow.

"This is a mighty fine spot here," he said quietly.

"I think it's pretty nice, too."

"I've got a question for you."

"All right," Jane said.

"I was wondering if you'd mind if I gave you a kiss."

She smiled. "I wouldn't mind."

Ton closed his eyes, leaned in, and for a few beautiful moments all the world's troubles slipped away.

"Thank you," he said afterward, smiling.

"You're welcome."

They gently turned to lay on their backs again, Jane's head once more on Ton's shoulder, a hand resting on his heart. They talked, relaxed and easy-like, until their eyes got heavy. As Jane nearly nodded off, she realized she had to go.

"I need to get back," she said.

"I'll go with you."

"You don't need to. I'll be alright."

"Don't be silly. It's still dark. No one will see us. We can wind our way through the outskirts of town to the ranch."

"Okay," she agreed.

Neither of them knew that from the bunkhouse Ben had seen Jane leave. He'd gone directly back to the ranch to rouse Mr. Witherspoon. Mr. Witherspoon sent Ben to Ton's, assuming that Jane had headed there. When Ben had returned with no sign of Ton or Jane, Mr. Witherspoon decided to wait on the porch for Jane's return, getting angrier by the minute.

Ton and Jane didn't see him until they'd made it nearly all the way up to the house. By then Mr. Witherspoon stood on the porch, glaring down at them. Ton looked Mr. Witherspoon in the eye. He was startled, sure, but he felt good about having come up by way of the front of the house. He didn't like sneaking around. He would have to confront her father soon enough—may as well be now.

"Jane," Mr. Witherspoon said firmly, "come here."

"Pa." Her voice was hushed.

"Where have you been?"

"Hello, sir," Ton intervened, tipping his cap, "My name's Ton Fish, and Jane and I had a talk on Arsenal Hill."

"Well, you can get on out of here," Mr. Witherspoon replied. "And I recommend you never come back. Now Jane, get inside."

"I love your daughter, sir," Ton said. "You can't keep that from being so. And I'm hoping she'll love me back."

"You don't know my daughter. And if you loved her, you'd have already converted," Mr. Witherspoon retorted. "Now, Jane, I'm going to say this only one more time. Come inside."

Jane looked at Ton longingly, but he knew that, for then, he had to let her go. So he did.

Chapter 9

It rattled Ton to have things break the way they did with Jane. For the next few days he came to work distracted, didn't say much, didn't have his usual smile or bounce. Perhaps this was a factor in the ensuing accident.

It occurred late in the morning, a few days after he'd met Jane on Arsenal Hill. Ton had slid underneath a flat-bed rail car filled with lumber to complete patchwork on hose and pipe separations in its brake system. Satisfied with the patch job, Ton went to couple the car he'd fixed with another. Coupling is dangerous anytime, and on this occasion it was doubly so because Ton had to lean back to make sure his head didn't get whacked by one of the long slabs of lumber hanging off the back. He was holding his head and chest farther back than usual, then, unable to see his hands while he reached for the drawheads as the car he'd repaired edged toward the one he aimed to couple it with. As difficult as the maneuver was, as the cars came within inches of each other, Ton actually thought he'd pegged it right. Suddenly, though, he felt a drawhead smash into his hand. He immediately tried to pull his hand away, but he felt bones on his fingers getting crushed. He let out a yell. He pulled harder, felt more crunching, and screamed in pain again. Finally, he got his hand free.

He saw that he had two utterly smashed and mangled fingers, dangling kind of crookedly. Another brakeman had rushed over. He could barely look at Ton's hand.

"That'll do for today," Ton said grimacing.

Trying to ignore the pain, he mounted his horse one-handed and made his way downtown to the Rio Grande's lead physician, Dr. Samuel Pinkerton. By the time he reached the receptionist at the doc's office, Ton's face was white, his injured hand covered in blood. The receptionist gave him a towel and led him directly to Dr. Pinkerton's office.

"This doesn't look good," the doctor said frankly. "You'll have to spend the night in the hospital. To be honest, I'll be surprised if we can save these two fingers."

For some reason, New York's *The World* would report that Ton had returned to Manhattan to have the procedure done, but the truth is Dr. Pinkerton, after seeing that blood flow was virtually nonexistent and fearing the onset of gangrene, cut the fingers himself the next day.

Dr. Pinkerton removed Ton's entire index finger and a good portion of his middle finger. Post-op the doctor told Ton that if by the next afternoon he looked to be healing satisfactorily, he could go on his way.

***

That next night, after getting released from the hospital, Ton went to the Cannon Ball saloon. He hung up his Prince Albert coat—which he couldn't wear properly over his slung arm anyhow—found Walters and a few other pals from out East, and immediately threw back a couple of shots. The belts didn't keep him from feeling heartsick over Jane, but they did help numb his hand a little. The longer the evening went on, the less Ton felt he could rely on his medication to keep the pain at bay.

"How's the hand, Ton?" Walters asked.

"Darn paw is throbbing."

"Ah, but it was only a couple of fingers," Charles, one of the fellas, said.

Ton laughed. "Yeah, well, I think the morphine is wearing off."

"I've got some at my apartment," Charles said.

"That should do the trick," Ton said.

"I'll be right back."

Charles returned within minutes and put a small bottle of laudanum, a form of morphine, on the table. Ton swallowed a dose, and then another.

This was before any real regulation of the pharmaceutical industry, a time during which you could go down to a local drugstore and purchase morphine just as you would crackers. Drugstore owners, in fact, advertised its availability in newspapers right alongside ads for soap.

Anyway, it didn't take long for the additionnal morphine to help Ton's hand feel better. He relaxed a little, and by and by, a dice game began. At first, it was a low-money affair between Ton, Walters, Charles, and a couple other fellows they knew from the rails, but before long a couple of guys they didn't know asked to join the action.

With Ton rolling, the newcomers immediately found themselves on the wrong end of two come-outs. Well, these guys must've been emboldened by the "who-hit-John" they'd been sipping, because straightaway they went to protesting. They declared that a one-armed man shouldn't be allowed to roll dice, suggesting the game wasn't on the level.

"Best watch it before I show you what a one-armed man can do," Ton threatened.

"I demand a new roller," one of 'em replied.

"No new roller," Ton said. "Now pay up."

"The son of his father says pay up, huh? Well, I say this game's been rigged by you dudes. Something doesn't add up here. I say switch rollers you one-armed bandit."

These guys were apparently serious. They were standing now, bellicose-like, and taking their money off the table. At that, quick as a whip, Ton stood and grabbed the back of his chair with his good arm, and—in what seemed like one motion—brought the chair down upon the fast-talker's head. The waylaid man's sidekick then chucked a glass of beer at Ton. It struck him on the head, but Ton barely felt its affect, what with the whiskey and morphine. Shoot, at that point, Ton probably could've shrugged off a whole keg hitting him.

Ton charged after the beer-chucker, plowed into him with his left shoulder, and knocked him to the ground. Worried about Ton's hand, Walters and Charles stepped in to break it up. They had to darn near bear-hug Ton before they could get him to settle down. The fast-talker and his friends eased off. They didn't seem to have any more wind in them for a fight after Ton's rush. They watched as Ton's friends guided him outside.

As they walked, Ton seemed to be cooling down. But then they came abreast the Bower residence, near State Street, and a dog came running from the yard toward them, barking like a maniac.

"Get outta here," Ton hollered at the dog.

Ton was a dog lover, so for him to lash out like that was perhaps the clearest sign that the morphine and alcohol had knocked him off-kilter. As I say, he loved his dog Chuck Jr., and growing up, his Skye terrier Charlie was probably his best friend. Later, training as Rough Riders in San Antonio, I saw Ton bust into a circle of gamblers huddled around a dog fight and save a wounded dog. He took that dog back to camp, and it became the Rough Riders' mascot. But he lashed out at the Bower dog this night in Utah.

Walters guided Ton toward a strip of grass bordering State Street and said, "Let's take a seat, cool off for a minute."

As they did so, a copper walked up. Perhaps he'd heard Ton lash out at the Bowers' dog and figured that Ton was in a bad way. Whatever it was, the copper—a sergeant, no less—came up by Ton's side, reached down, and kind of nudged him on the shoulder to check on him.

"Don't hurt my hand or I'll tell Pinkerton on you," Ton said sardonically.

The sergeant, probably tired from a long night and in no mood for smartness, apparently took Ton's Pinkerton comment as a reference to the detective agency, rather than Ton's doctor. "What are you talking about?" he asked.

"What do you mean, what am I talking about? Just don't hurt the hand, you hear? Or you'll have someone coming for you," Ton replied.

On the spot, the sergeant decided to haul Ton to the station, where he could sober up for a few hours, hopefully learn his lesson, and then be on his way. But Ton refused to get up, and when the sergeant moved in to take hold of Ton's arm, Ton resisted. Walters tried to calm the copper and get Ton to comply, but neither approach worked. The two began to scuffle a bit, only between his injury, the whiskey, and the morphine, Ton was in no condition to take on the sergeant. Sure enough, in a matter of seconds Ton found himself with his good arm behind his back, chicken-wing pinned.

"I'm Pinkerton," Ton said, trying to bring up Dr. Pinkerton again but making little sense, and confusing the cop into thinking Ton was saying that he was a Pinkerton detective.

Rather than respond, the sergeant simply marched

Ton toward the jailhouse. But Ton wasn't through yet.

"What's your name and number?" he demanded. "I'll have your head, too, before this thing is over."

"You need to sober up, young man. Plain and simple." To his credit, the sergeant refused to get drawn in.

The minute he was locked up, Ton fell asleep on a cot.

Later the next day, rested and sobered up, he had a chance to mull matters, and he wasn't proud of himself. He apologized to Sergeant Wire and the other coppers on duty, and he made it a point to apologize in-person to the Bowers and their dog. He knew word of his arrest and his scuffle with a copper would spread pretty quickly throughout Salt Lake. And he knew this would make it that much harder to convince Elder Witherspoon that he was the right man for his daughter.

He decided he needed to get away from Salt Lake City, to give Jane space, to allow them to both do some living, and in the process perhaps find a better way for them to end up together. Within a matter of days, then, he entrusted Walters with a letter for Jane and caught a train back east.

Dear Jane,

I hope this finds you happy and well. As I leave town, I wanted to let you know that I'm embarrassed about my behavior the other night. For what it is worth, I have made my apologies.

As we have discussed, we both have a lot of living to do. I do no want to stand between you and your family. I take solace in knowing that you have a mighty spirit, Jane. Do not lose that fire.

Sincerely,

Ton Fish

Chapter 10

Ton returned to New York in the fall of 1896, a few days before the presidential election between McKinley and Bryan. By then, I'd moved up from newsboy to cub reporter and grown a few inches.

It was Sunday, late morning, when we learned of Ton's return. I'd come home from work for a quick lunch break when there was a knock at the door. My mom answered and, even though she knew I'd worked for Ton in the past, was shocked to find him standing there. To her, the Fish family amounted to American royalty. Her world and theirs just didn't collide.

I came to the door.

"Hey there, old boy, what do you say?" Ton asked.

"Great to see you, Ton," I said, smiling big as we shook hands. "Come in, come in."

My mom put on some coffee.

"My you've grown, Rory Mac. Look at you," Ton said.

I was nearing six feet tall, but my frame remained Abe Lincoln-skinny.

"How've you been, Ton?" I asked.

"Well, I had quite an adventure out West, but I'm back in the city for now. Got my right hand rather smashed, though, so no boxing." He held it up.

"My goodness." It was still rather mangled looking.

We stepped over to sit at the table.

"Oh, it's fine now. I've got something here for you," Ton said, reaching into his Prince Albert. "I was thinking of you, about how you were my favorite second and all. And, well, seeing as I can't box anymore, I thought maybe you and I could at least go to a bout."

He handed me two tickets to the Maher vs. Choynski fight at the Broadway Athletic Club. I'd been following the pre-fight coverage for weeks, as had all of New York, never imagining that I'd be able to attend. I smiled even bigger.

"You want to go?" Ton asked.

"You bet! It'll be something." My mom brought us some coffee as we took a seat.

Ton explained how he'd lost his fingers, and how things had gone with Jane. He described Utah's mountains and the Arizona desert and what it was like to camp in Apache territory. Before returning to New York, in fact, he'd visited the Lewishon mine again, supposedly to check on his investment, but really—I'd learn later—to see if he could drown his sorrows in booze. This would explain the dark, albeit faint, circles under his eyes and a kind of weariness about him that was unusual. Looking back later, I realized that he was wrestling with addiction. He'd managed to wean himself off the morphine, but in the process had taken to the drink even more.

As we talked, my mom pampered us, bringing out shortbread and refilling our mugs. She wanted to make Ton comfortable, and I knew she enjoyed hearing about his adventures. It warmed my heart to see how happy it made her to receive a member of the Fish family.

By and by, we got to talking about the upcoming election. Ton couldn't believe that my paper, *The World*, had come out for McKinley, while Hearst's *Journal* had come out for Bryan. *The World*, after all, was known for catering to the working man and had generally been associated with the Democratic Party. But Pulitzer thought Bryan was too enamored with free silver, so his paper backed a Republican—which is what likely motivated

Hearst, Pulitzer's yellow rival, to come out for Bryan. That's just the way this election was; wild and woolly and unpredictable, the whole thing magnificent theater.

Ton said he disliked that Republican big-money folks were bankrolling McKinley, and he liked Bryan's common-folks appeal. But, like Pulitzer, he didn't think Bryan's plan to use both silver and gold to back the dollar added up. He also didn't like the anti-immigrant strain running through the Democratic Party, which, as a son of Irish immigrants and a Catholic, I could relate to.

For Ton, there was also the issue of family history—the Fishes had been strong Union men, and therefore strong Republicans. Ton's grandfather, in fact, had helped raise an all-black regiment during the Civil War. Taken altogether, Ton leaned McKinley's way. So did I.

Ultimately, of course, McKinley won, and it was under him that Ton and I would fight in Cuba. But Cuba didn't factor much into the election. Ton—partial to the rebellion—might've been following reports on the Cuban struggle against Spanish rule, but most Americans still weren't focused on it. Shoot, the yellows didn't even yet support the idea of the United States actively siding with the Cuban rebels. *The World's* view well into 1897 was that the Cubans could win independence on their own, provided we allow their merchant vessels to trade at American ports. Hearst's *Journal* felt similarly, despite the legend later immortalized in the film *Citizen Kane*.

This legend holds that in January 1897, journalist Richard Harding Davis and painter Frederick Remington—both of whom Hearst had sent to Havana—wired a report to Hearst that all was quiet in Cuba, and in turn Hearst cabled back, "Please remain. You furnish the pictures, and I'll furnish the war." It's a good story and a great line. It's just not true.

Anyway, rather than Cuba, monetary policy drove the 1896 election. Folks gobbled up books on money by the thousands, books like *Coin's Financial School* and its rebuttal, *Coin's Financial Fool*. Generally, the issue broke along sectional lines: those in the North and East, where manufacturing and finance reigned, wanted American money to be backed only by gold. This would keep inflation down. Farmers in the South and West wanted both silver and gold to underpin the dollar, to inflate the prices of their crops.

As I say, Bryan championed bimetallism with vigor, like when he declared at the Democratic convention, "You shall not crucify mankind upon a cross of gold." But factions within the Democratic Party were split over the issue.

In the meantime, the Republican Party was less divided over the question. So McKinley, conducting his campaign from his front porch as Bryan barnstormed across the country, struck a moderate stance by embracing gold and trying to rally folks around a protective tariff. Ultimately, the strategy worked.

***

The election was over by the time Ton and I met back up for the Choynski-Maher fight. I took a streetcar to the corner of Broadway and Old London, which was filled with folks heading to the fight. For years, a cast of politicians and other Gotham do-gooders had outlawed boxing in the city. But now it was back, and you could feel the anticipation in the air.

As Ton and I stepped into the cinderbox building that the Broadway Athletic Club called home, the energy tearing through the place was even more powerful. And this was just the undercard.

Tobacco smoke hung heavily in the air but I could still get a broad look at the mix of men in the crowd, many of them in bowlers and topcoats. They were packed in tight and steep—the bleachers rose nearly straight upward against the walls, at such an angle that it looked dangerous for those sitting at the top.

Seated one box over from Ton and me was Teddy Roosevelt, at this time the city's police commissioner. He told the press after the fights that he'd attended as an overseer, to make sure the law wasn't trampled upon. To be fair, he did step in to stop a fight on the undercard because he thought it was too brutal. But I think he also just wanted to watch good boxing. He loved the sport and made that clear enough when he told a reporter later that night, "I don't care very much for professional sport of any kind, but I thoroughly believe in boxing, exactly as I believe in football and other manly games."

As for the main fight, it was a tough, bruising affair. Both fighters uncorked haymakers, but in the sixth round Maher landed three particularly powerful blasts, the last of which left Choynski unconscious and quivering on the mat. The Irish had their win.

On our way out, Ton brought me by Mr. Roosevelt's box seat to say hello. Teddy was a family friend who held the Fish legacy in high esteem and saw the family as an ally. He met us energetically and called the fight "bully." Then he scoffed at the complaints that he knew would be thrown his way in the morning papers, on account of the main event having ended with such a brutal knockout. He didn't want to hear it. "I got knocked out in polo on two separate occasions for longer than Choynski departed us tonight," he told us.

He knew what the critics' talking points would be already. Religious men would rip the sport for being inhumane and point out that gamblers associated with boxing. Others would say boxing was a stigma upon our civilization, a disgrace to the city, and a reflection of defect in American government. Most everyone I knew, though, considered the fight "bully."

On our way home from the bout, Ton and I stopped off at Gilsey's café to meet with some of Ton's friends and rehash the fight. This was my first time inside the place. Amid the ornately carved woodwork, the chiffon draping, and the gilt bronze chandeliers, I mostly just listened to Ton and his buddies as they talked about the fight, politics, and even the Cuban rebellion, which was starting to get more attention in the press, especially in the yellows.

We talked about Ton's new job, too. He'd recently been hired at Brown Brothers, an investment banking and trading company. He didn't seem all that enthused about it, though.

"Too much sitting," he said. "It doesn't matter if I'm analyzing a financial statement or buying opportunities, I'm still sitting. You know what I mean? I'm penned up all day reading balance sheets and looking at spreads." He looked my way. "I don't know, Rory, sometimes I think doing what you're doing would be better. You're out on the street, getting information, moving, acting."

"We'll trade wages, then," I said, laughing.

"Look, I can help someone buy a railroad with three-percent bonds, when not too long ago they would've had to pay seven or eight percent, but what about it?" Ton asked. "It doesn't get me going. I'm young; I want to get out." He paused. "Mr. Harriman says, 'I think this is a good time to buy some money.' And it truly gets him excited. But it just doesn't do it for me."

"Sounds like we've got a money man decrying money," Pat teased.

"Nah. Look, I know what capital can do," Ton said. "It's just that mastering money flows and scouring data doesn't inspire me."

As the night wore on, I noticed that Ton was getting pretty soaked. By the time we left, he was sideways. Pat and I made sure he made it to back to 53 Irving Place all right, but seeing his drinking close up rattled me. He'd gone West with such enthusiasm, only to return with an ailing heart and a malformed hand that didn't allow him to box. And he had those dark circles under his eyes. The buoyancy he'd had when we first met seemed deflated.

Chapter 11

I felt even more unsettled about Ton a few weeks later, after *The World* sent me out to drum up some information on a Tammany man who was caught up in a nasty divorce that involved infidelity and theft—you know, low-down kind of stuff. I'd learned that a good place to start with such matters was a private detective who specialized in divorce, a guy named Sharkey. I'd gotten information from him here and there in the past, and I knew that he frequented the bars on the edge of Hell's Kitchen, around West Thirty-fourth and Ninth Avenue, especially the Erhardt Brothers' saloon.

Around ten o'clock at night, I stepped inside Erhardts' and was surprised to find Ton sitting at a table with two women, a Mrs. Mable Phelps and another dame, all of them cavorting and carrying on, cozy-like. It struck me as odd; this wasn't the type of place society hung out in. I came over to say hello and saw straightaway that whisky had bent Ton pretty good. I recognized both the ladies from the neighborhood. They were known for playing things loose; neither was up to any good, in my view.

"Hey there, Rory Mac," Ton said, smiling too big and acting overly cheerful, like folks can do when the whisky gets too deep. "Have a seat, join us."

The ladies smiled at me. I smirked. I was already trying to figure out a way to ease Ton out of there, as opposed to making a scene by trying to get him to leave straightaway. I pulled up a chair. We chatted for a few minutes about nothing and the ladies flirted with Ton— they were really laying it on—when, just as I was about to make an excuse for Ton and me to exit, Sharkey walked in.

Now, Sharkey was a morose kind of guy who drank a lot, and had a mean, jealous streak in him when it came to ladies, maybe from all the divorce work he did. Anyway, unbeknownst to me—or Ton, for that matter—he'd recently taken up some sort of arrangement with Mrs. Phelps, who claimed that her first husband had run out on her years prior. So he didn't take well to seeing her sitting at a table with Ton and me, all smiles. He stepped up quick, and I could tell he was hot. *This isn't good*, I thought.

Ton seemed oblivious. He asked Sharkey if he'd like to sit down for a drink. "I've drawn a tab," Ton said, glancing over at the check he'd already laid on the table.

"Who says your credit's any good?" Sharkey said, clearly not aware that he was talking to a Fish. He turned to a waitress who happened to be walking by and said, motioning to Ton, "I wouldn't take a check from this lout."

"Where do you get off…?" Ton said, standing up.

But before he could finish the sentence, I hopped up, grabbed him by the shoulders, and started driving him toward the door.

"We were just leaving," I said, turning back toward the waitress. "Check's on the table. Fill it out proper."

We walked for a few blocks without saying much. I was worried about him. When I was a bit older and a little wiser, I could see how Ton's injury, the morphine, the drinking, and losing Jane could've gotten him started down this dark path. It wasn't horrible yet, mind you, as far as the drinking went, but it was enough to make me worry. And it was affecting his confidence. He appeared untethered and uncertain, and it made me feel that way, too. I didn't like it one bit. I decided I needed to find a way to pick him up.

***

Having chewed on it for a few days, I settled on a plan and humped it over to the Madsen, a high-ennd hotel-like residence for bachelors, then up several floors, to Ton's place.

"Hey there, Rory Mac," Ton answered the door.

"Sorry to bother you at home," I said, "but I have a couple of questions for you."

"No bother at all, old boy. Come on in."

We stepped inside and he grabbed me a glass of water, with ice—one of the perks of living in a place like the Madsen.

"What do you say?" Ton asked.

"Well, it's just that I've been thinking about getting in the ring," I said, a little nervous. "And I was wondering if you wouldn't mind maybe training me."

"You want to box?"

"I do. What do you say?"

"I think it's a fine idea," Ton said, his face brightening. "Of course I'll do it." I could tell he really did like the idea, and this brought a smile to my face. "We can train at the Metropolitan Club or perhaps the Union League," he added. "You're serious about this, now?"

"I am."

"I tell you, it sounds swell, Rory Mac."

He'd meant what he said, because within days, Ton had us set up to train at the Union League—the most prestigious men's club in the nation, with the finest gym. It was formed in 1863 by a group of men led by the Fishes and the Stuyvesants, who were tired of their previous club's weak support of Lincoln in the Civil War. The newly-formed club outfitted two black regiments to fight for the Union Army. This kept with family tradition—Ton's great-grandfather led the movement to abolish slavery in New York in 1799, and Ton's grandfather signed the Fifteenth Amendment, which gave blacks the vote. Along with the Fishes, the Union League counted among its members men like J. P. Morgan, John D. Rockefeller, and the former president, Ulysses S. Grant. It was said that the combined wealth of its members amounted to about a trillion dollars. And it was no surprise when, in 1883, the club spent big money building its new headquarters—the nation's first purpose-built structure for a gentlemen's club—on the northeast corner of Fifth Avenue and Thirty-ninth Street. Inside, the level of luxury set the standard for the flurry of gentlemen's club buildings commissioned in its wake.

This is where I launched my boxing career.

Ton took my training seriously. He scheduled our workouts for early in the morning, before I had to report to work. He said that this was the best time to train. He lent me a couple of books on the greats, like the bantam standout Terry McGovern and heavyweight Jim Corbett. Both men, I came to learn, stressed the importance of eating heartily and avoiding tobacco and alcohol, the last of which I found a little ironic since it was Ton who'd given me the book.

Ton did most of the exercises with me. We'd start workouts with sit-ups, only fifty at first, adding five more each day till we'd worked our way to two hundred. We'd do toe touches and back bends while holding light dumbbells. After, we'd get on the Union League's pulley machines. At first, I did pulley exercises with only small amounts of weight, but as the weeks passed I was pulling more and more. Corbett was big on handstands, too, so Ton would have us do them for a few minutes. Then we'd put the gloves on.

We'd start glove training with the light bag, for only about three minutes at first. Within several weeks, I could do five, three-minute rounds in succession, with a minute's rest between each. Some days we'd work on the heavy bag. We'd often spar lightly at the end of our workout, focusing on technique. In the early days of our training, it could hardly be called sparring, though, because Ton had to explain everything to me, from getting into a proper stance to carrying out the simplest of combinations.

It was slow going, but in time my stance became second nature. We spent days focused on making sure I held my head properly. The key was to avoid offering a "full face" to an opponent's attack. Eventually we practiced some lead jabs with the left and some close-quarter work with the right. But, as I say, we progressed slowly.

As the weeks ran along and we settled into a rhythm of getting up early and training hard, I saw Ton getting his zeal back. It's not as if he got better right away or stopped drinking outright. And it wasn't something we talked about. But his step became bouncier, and his eyes brighter. I suspected there were nights he still drank too much, and there were times he still seemed downbeat, as if a certain kind of melancholy was haunting him, but I remember thinking one morning that the old Ton Fish was coming back.

The timing was just right. For that very afternoon, William Randolph Hearst paid me a visit, setting in motion an adventure for Ton and me the likes of which we couldn't have fathomed.

Chapter 12

I was on the trail of a Tammany political hack's young mistress, tasked with finding out if she had heard any political scuttle during pillow-talk. I'd staked out near a small grocery, across from where the mistress lived. As I leaned back against the wall of the grocery, scanning a newspaper, a fellow in a long, dark overcoat and top hat came up and stood alongside me, with his back against the wall, too. I glanced over at him quickly, half-wondering why someone with such nice clothes would hang out in these parts, before going back to my newspaper.

"You waitin' on Sally Ann, huh?" he asked, barely even nodding my way.

"Just reading *The World*," I said.

"Well this paper's better," the man said, reaching into a side pocket and handing me the *Journal*. I laughed a little.

"I'm good with *The World*," I said, looking up at the man. My eyes widened when I recognized the long face and deep-set eyes. I looked again to be sure. It was indeed William Randolph Hearst. I swallowed a lump in my throat.

"Hello, sir," I said, putting out my hand. "I'm Rory Mac."

"I know who you are. Nice to meet you," he said. I couldn't believe he knew my name.

"You too, sir."

"I'll get right to it, Rory Mac. I came here to hire you. I want you to become an investigator for the *Journal*. What do you say?"

I hadn't expected this.

"Well, sir, I don't know, I mean haven't thought about it. I guess I'll have to chew on it."

"I'll give you till tomorrow," Hearst said, in a way that let me know that was just the way it'd be. Tomorrow or never.

"What are the terms? And will I be able to write?"

"Yes, you can write," he said. "As for the pay, $450 a year."

My heart jumped. That was a ton of money to me. Still, I sensed something in Hearst's voice that made me think he'd even go higher.

"$500. No less," I said, a little surprised to actually hear myself say it. Hearst thought for a moment.

"All right, let me know," he said.

I nodded and glanced ahead, letting him know that Sally Ann was coming toward us. Understanding, he started down the street in the opposite direction.

I can't remember if I got anything of value out of my conversation with Sally Ann. I do know my head was reeling. A yearly sum of $500 would change everything for my mom. That I could not ignore. I figured if *The World* couldn't match the offer, I'd have to go to the *Journal*, plain and simple. When I talked with Ton about it, he agreed. "Rory, it's bully," he kept saying.

I met with *The World's* Ike White to talk about my current pay. Going into the meeting, I'd wondered if he wouldn't mind seeing a young up-and-comer go—less competition for him. Sure enough, while he did try to convince me that it was better to stay at *The World*, his effort seemed halfhearted. He offered a modest raise, but it certainly didn't match Hearst's offer. He went on about the *Journal* being a terrible place to work and claimed that Hearst lacked ethics.

After a few minutes, I'd had my fill. I stood up, reached out my hand, and said matter-of-factly, "It's been nice working for you, sir." Then I walked over to the *Journal's* offices, also on Newspaper Row in lower Manhattan.

***

I'd heard that if he wasn't out investigating an angle, you could find Mr. Hearst in the office, on the same floor as his journalists, analyzing the latest stories. That's exactly where I found him. A secretary had checked to make sure it was all right to let me into the newsroom and then led me in. Mr. Hearst stepped over to shake my hand.

As he approached, I saw a thirty-five-year-old man who was willing to take risks, who had vim in his step and oozed ebullience, the type of guy that made me think, *whatever he's doing, I'd like to do, too.*

It was surreal. Hearst was the man everyone in the industry was talking about. He'd been raised in affluence in California after his father, a geologist, had struck gold in 1849. His mother was a polished schoolteacher. She'd wanted her boy to have the best education money could buy, so she put him in private schools, made sure he traveled abroad. In 1881, Hearst graduated from the same Eastern prep school from which Ton would graduate in 1890, the renowned St. Paul's in New Hampshire. Harvard came next. And now here he was, operating the most low-down—as the elites might've characterized it—yellow in the world.

It took a bit to get used to the idea that I now worked for him. But in many ways, my days weren't all that different. And I still got up early to train with Ton. I got nervous a few weeks into the gig, though, when Hearst called me to his office. The summons immediately made me think about the warnings that Ike White had given me before I left *The World.*

"Rory Mac," Hearst said as I stepped in. He was standing to the side of his desk, looking over some papers. "How's it going?" he asked, reaching out to shake my hand.

"I'm good, sir," I said. Hearst walked behind his desk, took a seat, and looked upward for a few moments, sort of toward the ceiling, like he was thinking about something.

"I've got something for you," he finally said. "What do you think about going to Cuba?"

I thought of the stories coming out of Cuba, of the atrocities, the suffering, the rebels' courage. The situation had been attracting more and more ink, especially in the *Journal.* So I knew this request was important.

"Cuba?"

"Yes."

"When do I leave, and what would like me to do there?" I asked.

Hearst smiled. "I knew you'd be in. I've got a journalist coming into town tomorrow from the Washington bureau. Name's Karl Decker. Meet him here tomorrow, late morning, and he'll fill you in on the details."

"Yes, sir. Thank you."

That night I told Ton about it. He thought the idea of me going to Cuba to cover the rebellion was among the wildest, most adventurous things he'd ever heard. "Ah, you're living, old boy," Ton said. "You're in the arena, Rory Mac. Good on you."

***

Karl Decker was middle-aged, on the tall side, and

a bit round, with a thick mustache which curved upward at the ends. He shook my hand firmly and said, "Karl Decker."

"Good to meet you, sir."

"Have you been briefed?"

"Not entirely."

He walked me into a private office, motioned for me to have a seat, shut the door, and sat down behind a desk.

"This will be like no other assignment you've ever been on," he explained. "Tomorrow, ten o'clock in the morning, I'm traveling to Cuba. The Spanish know I'm coming. Ostensibly, I'm going there to investigate the Evangelina Castilla affair. But really I'm going to lay the groundwork to spring her from prison."

My eyes popped. I knew of the Castilla story—two Cuban sisters, both reportedly beautiful, imprisoned by the Spanish along with their father, a rebel. Decker had my full attention.

Continuing, he said, "Once I'm comfortable with our ability to execute the plan, I will send for you."

"All right." I nodded my head slowly, a little in shock.

"This, of course, must be guarded with the utmost secrecy," Decker said. "As it stands now, in addition to me and you, only Mr. Hearst and a secret contact in Cuba know about this. Understood?"

"Yes, sir."

"Good. Now, in putting this plan together, I told Mr. Hearst I needed a young, street-smart person, with a slight build and guts, who can leave on a moment's notice. That's why we're talking now. He says you can be trusted. Is this so?" He looked at me intently.

"Yes, it is."

"Spain doesn't just have spies in Havana. They have them here in New York, too. So secrecy is crucial."

"I understand."

"At some point in the coming days, at this building, you will receive a secret message from a hand-picked courier. This message will contain the time of departure for the ship you'll be taking to Cuba. You'll find this ship on the East River's southernmost dock. The captain of this ship is a friend of our operation, but he will have only limited knowledge of what we're actually doing. Got it?"

"Yes, sir." I rose, sensing the dismissal. "I look forward to receiving the message."

"One more thing," Decker said, stopping me short.

"Yes?"

"As I've mentioned to Mr. Hearst, we may need another man, someone with a bigger, stronger build. I'll know more in a week or so. We will have some help in Cuba, but we need Americans to do the bulk of the work springing her. That way, if we get caught, we have a good chance of getting extradited—at least I hope. If a Cuban were to be caught, they would likely be killed, quickly and discreetly. Plus, Hearst wants to make sure folks know, if we're successful, that the *Journal* pulled this off. If there's someone you trust who fits the bill, please report to me directly with your recommendation first thing tomorrow morning."

"I will, sir."

I immediately, of course, thought of Ton. To him, the prospect of joining an effort to spring Evangelina Castilla from prison would be thrilling.

Chapter 13

Over the previous few weeks, Evangelina's story had become known throughout America, thanks largely to the *Journal*. The scenario had started two years earlier, in 1895, just as the Cuban rebellion was starting. Evangelina's father, on a mission with a group of rebels to harass Spanish positions, walked into an ambush and was captured and imprisoned. Evangelina and her sister, Carmen, were distraught. Day after day, they walked to their father's prison to plead for his release. But day after day, they met rebuke.

Several gut-wrenching months passed until one day the sisters received horrible news: their father had been sentenced to death. Upon hearing this, Evangelina and Carmen walked to their father's prison, collapsed into a heap on the ground, and wept. At this seemingly hopeless moment, fate intervened. The son of Cuba's presiding general in Havana happened to walk by. Moved by the sobbing sisters on the ground, he inquired about matters and decided to help.

Ultimately, although the sisters did not secure their father's release, they managed to get his death sentence commuted. There was a condition: that they accompany their father to a less rigorous jailhouse on a tiny island off the mainland—the Isle of Pines, a remote place from which there would be little chance of escape and even less opportunity to cause the Spanish government any trouble.

Relieved, the Castilla sisters happily went to the Isle of Pines with their father. During their first month there, they appreciated how simple life was. Evangelina and Carmen settled into their roles as their father's housekeepers and enjoyed the island's peaceful rhythms, which were in step with the soft waves that steadily lapped its calm and sandy shores. Upon completing their daily chores, the sisters would take walks on the piazza, read and relax in rocking chairs on the front porch, and swim in the warm ocean water. In the evening, when their father returned home from a day of conscripted labor, they would dote on him. This was a far cry from the uncertainty and danger in Havana.

Within several weeks, however, the peaceful rhythms of life on the island were jolted. The Isle of Pines' lax military governor, Governor Menendez, was replaced by Colonel Jose Berriz, a short and unattractive man with menacing green eyes, bushy hair, and black whiskers that crept up his cheeks. He was not only a favorite of General Weyler, known as "The Butcher," but a known Butcher-wannabe—and the nephew of Spain's prime minister. The men on the island had taken immediate notice of the Castilla sisters' striking beauty. But it was Berriz who decided that Evangelina had to be his.

Mesmerized by Evangelina's beauty, Colonel Berriz rode by the Castilla residence on horseback and found her sitting in a rocking chair on the porch. "There is the prettiest little rebel of the war," he said loudly. Uncomfortable with Berriz's tone and demeanor, Evangelina stood up and walked inside. She could hear Berriz laughing as he rode off.

The next day, Berriz knocked at the Castillas' front door. Evangelina answered. She was surprised to see him standing there.

"Hello Evangelina," he said.

"Hello," she said, spooked.

"This is very comfortable for a prison, no?"

"It is," Evangelina warily replied.

Berriz looked her over suggestively. "I make it as easy as I can for prisoners, and might do more. But I observe no sign of gratitude."

"The prisoners are grateful for your clemency," Evangelina replied.

"I hate to lock people up. Is the governor to be the only one to suffer?" he asked, looking at her longingly.

"My father's calling," a desperate Evangelina lied. "Have a good day, sir."

She closed the door gently and hurried to her room.

His advances rebuffed, the next day Berriz directed one of his men to arrest Evangelina's father and place him in the Protectorado, the Isle of Pines' harsher prison.

A tearful Evangelina went to this desolate place, as Berriz had expected, and pleaded with the prison guards to release her father. They instructed her to go see Col. Berriz. Reluctant but desperate, she did.

Upon entering the colonel's office, she asked, "Why is my father in the Protectorado?"

Colonel Berriz called for an assistant and ordered him to have her father immediately released. "As long as your father has you to intercede on his behalf, he will not face such troubles," he said, eyeing her. "I can refuse you nothing, Evangelina. You will come to me again, however, and I will judge your gratitude."

It came as a great relief to the sisters when their father returned home, but Evangelina was still worried. That night she told her father and Carmen all that had happened with Colonel Berriz. Mr. Castilla shook his head in sadness. He knew the matter would not end there.

Without saying anything, he got up and went to his room to fetch a knife he'd managed to hide. He gave it to

Evangelina and told her to never let it leave her side. "It is better to fight, for it is not hard to die, my Evangelina."

All was quiet for a couple of days. The Castillas tried to return to as normal a life as they could on the island. Meanwhile, Colonel Berriz, at first apparently confident that Evangelina would come to him, became increasingly agitated that she did not. When the third day arrived with still no visit from her, he became enraged and had the sisters' father secretly arrested again.

Later that night, Evangelina and Carmen, having enjoyed a day of light housekeeping, cooking, and strolling along the beach, waited for their father to return from work. As the hours passed and he did not arrive home, they became increasingly worried. They tried to sleep but neither could. As she lay down, Evangelina would occasionally peer out the front window, hoping to see her father walking up. Just before midnight, Evangelina went to check on Carmen and found her asleep. A short time later, looking out the front window and through the darkness, Evangelina saw someone approaching the house. At first she thought it was their father. But, looking closer, she tensed in dismay. It was not her father. It was Colonel Berriz, dressed in full uniform, gold lace on his shoulders and cap, stars on his collar, sword at his side, spurs on his boots.

He knocked, and for a moment, Evangelina froze. *Think*, she told herself, *think*. She knew instinctively what Berriz intended to do. And she realized that Berriz could easily force open the door and would do so if she were to hide. Once inside, if he didn't find her, he'd find her sister.

Carmen. I must keep Carmen safe. So, with Berriz still standing at the door, she rushed into Carmen's room and grabbed her sister's shoulders to wake her.

"Carmen, listen," she whispered. "Make no noise. Do you hear me?"

Startled, Carmen looked in Evangelina's eyes and nodded. Berriz knocked again. Evangelina stepped out into the hall but still did not answer. As she expected, he then forced his way in. There the two stood, staring at each other.

"You're surprised to see me," Berriz said.

"Have you come to tell me about my father?" Evangelina asked.

"I do him favors and yet get nothing in return. You can keep him free, Evangelina. You can protect him from the penal colonies in Africa. You know that?"

He moved in closer and tried to grab her hand.

"Where is my father?" she demanded, stepping backward.

"You have it in your power to make your father a free man." Berriz moved closer to her.

"In the name of your mother, your sister, leave me alone."

He laughed. "Do you think I have dressed myself as if for a princess's ball to come to a sermon by a little Cuban rebel?" He placed his face near her ear, pulled her tightly to him and said, "I love you."

Evangelina cried out and pulled away with all her might. Managing to break free, she dashed to her room. Berriz grabbed at her as she fled. Evangelina cried for help. Carmen, unable to stay still any longer, rushed out of her room to Evangelina.

Next door, Pablo Superville, a young prisoner, heard the commotion. He'd stepped outside out onto the street and within seconds two other men, prisoners as well, had done the same. These three men quickly made their way into the home. They rushed into Evangelina's room. Carmen was jumping on the back of Berriz, who was trying to force himself upon Evangelina. The men pounced.

Caught off guard and clearly outmanned, Berriz briefly tried to resist. The men overpowered him. Realizing that putting up a fight was useless, he settled on another tactic. As the island's chief military commander, he ordered Evangelina's rescuers out of the house. Disgusted, they bound him.

The men talked about killing Berriz, but they knew this would likely in turn get them executed. The gravity of the situation hit them when they realized this. They were holding the most powerful man on the island for attempted rape. Things could get difficult.

Rather than kill Berriz, they decided to march him to the island's chief judge, Don Enrique Gonzalez. Upon hearing this, Colonel Berriz broke down. Weeping, he begged like a child for them not to make him endure such an embarrassment, but they ignored him.

Seeing their indifference, Berriz hit upon another ploy.

"Murder! Murder!" he shouted, as loudly as he could. His captors tried to silence him, but he twisted violently away from them. They should've gagged him when they'd had the chance because he kept shouting "Murder! Murder! Murder!" hoping that the commotion would attract the attention of a few soldiers stationed down the road. In short order, it did just that. With their pistols drawn, the soldiers rushed to the scene.

Evangelina's rescuers had to think fast. They knew if the soldiers showed up and it became their word versus Berriz's, they would lose. So, just as the soldiers entered, they took flight through the bedroom window.

Seeing their boss bound, the soldiers rushed over to check on Colonel Berriz and untie his wrists. Freed, Colonel Berriz shouted, "Follow those murderers! Get them!" The soldiers followed their leader through the bedroom window in pursuit. Meanwhile, Carmen and Evangelina were left alone, huddled together, trembling and scared. They remained that way through the night, unsure of their father's whereabouts and Berriz's next move.

The next morning, two soldiers arrived to arrest Evangelina. They marched her and Carmen over to a Havana-bound vessel, the *Nuevo Cubano*. Just before being marched aboard, Evangelina was told that she faced charges of conspiracy against the Crown for luring Colonel Berriz into her bedroom as part of an elaborate plan to have him ambushed by men sympathetic to the rebel cause.

This was the story Berriz concocted, and this is how the Castilla sisters found themselves behind bars in Havana's infamous Casa de Recogidas prison. This is why, in mid-August, 1897, Evangelina came to be sentenced to twenty years of detainment in a former-castle-turned-harsh-prison in Ceuta, a Spanish possession in North Africa.

The *Journal* was the first to print the Castillas' story. Hearst had gotten a beat on it a month or two prior to the prison sentence, but he'd wanted to make sure his timing generated maximum effect. He figured that when the twenty-year sentence came down, the time was right. And my, was he correct. America became captivated with Evangelina's story. She came to embody all that was noble about the Cuban effort to win independence.

A more apt figure to represent the struggle, to reflect why America needed to support the downtrodden Cubans, it seemed, could hardly be conjured.

In the days and weeks ahead, the desire for information and updates was massive. Copy sold like hotcakes. In reading about the Castillas, Americans were introduced to new things, like the Isle of Pines and Havana's Casa de Recogidas prison, a filthy and harsh place which housed some of Cuba's most hardened female criminals. By extension, Americans became more interested in the Cuban rebellion, in trying to figure out exactly what was going on with their island neighbor.

Within a week or two of the *Journal* first printing Evangelina's story, women throughout New York State and beyond were signing petitions on her behalf. Julia Ward Howe, author of the "Battle Hymn of the Republic," wrote to His Holiness, Pope Leo XIII, asking him to intervene so that Evangelina would not have to endure an unfair and unprecedented twenty-year sentence. The prison sentence, according to Howe, was worse than death. The Pope even appealed to the Catholic Queen Regent of Spain to intervene.

Many within the Spanish government, however, responded to the hullabaloo by clinging to the story that Senorita Castilla was transferred to Havana because she'd participated in an assassination plot targeting Berriz; that she'd seductively lured him into her Isle of Pines prison home where he faced an ambush. Americans thought this sounded rather convenient and wondered where the trial had been.

Readers were appalled to learn that Evangelina and Carmen's Havana prison had a massive cage-like structure which served as the main holding area during the day. The prisoners were expected to simply hang out in this cage as passers-by on the street looked at them through wrought-iron bars, as if looking in on animals at the zoo. Crass men with their catcalls, ogling, and snide comments were the most humiliating. Irritated and angry, the prisoners oftentimes treated one another terribly. When Carmen was released a few weeks after the Castilla sisters' arrival, Evangelina, though happy for her sister, faced complete and utter despair. American papers covered all of this.

To quiet the uproar, Spanish authorities had Evangelina, and a handful of other political prisoners, moved to a more private space. This new cell, still within the Casa de Recogidas, also had better accommodations for bathing, and there Evangelina found more kinship and the freedom to do things like help illiterate prisoners with correspondence. At the same time General Weyler, "The Butcher," upset about the attention Evangelina's story had generated, ordered her incommunicado: she was not allowed to receive or to send any letters.

One of the few things to bring Evangelina solace, oddly enough, was the difficult work that the Casa de Recogidas asked of its prisoners. They scrubbed floors and outhouses. The work gave her a chance to take her mind off her despair. In addition, over time, she managed to develop a friendship with two women, a Señora Agramonte and a Miss Aguilar.

Still, life in the Casa de Recogidas was very difficult for Evangelina, especially given the uncertainties surrounding her potential transfer to North Africa and her father's fate. The prison warden didn't help either. One day, holding a copy of the *Journal*, he came over to Evangelina to show an article about her. "You have some fine friends," the warden said. "They will cry when you stand up before the soldiers with a bandage over your eyes and the word is given to shoot."

What Evangelina did not know was that these "friends" the warden spoke of—the yellows and American citizens—were rallying to her cause. This had likely slowed her transfer to North Africa. Ultimately, thanks to William Randolph Hearst, this is what would give her the best chance of being saved.

Chapter 14

When I told Ton about the mission, he picked me up in a bear hug, spun me around, and said, "My God, this is bully, Rory Mac. This is utterly spectacular. Oh, I've just got to go, old boy. I've just got to go."

I wasn't sure, though, how likely it was that Mr. Decker would ultimately request an additional man, let alone what the odds were of getting Decker to agree to Ton as the choice.

Walking to work after our boxing workout early the next morning, I thought about the best way to sell Decker on bringing Ton with us. I knew he'd have heard of Ton and the Fish family, but I couldn't determine whether notoriety would help Ton's cause or not. I decided I'd start with the qualities Ton possessed: courage, strength, a commitment to the cause. Then I'd drop his name.

At the office, after I'd given the character sketch to Mr. Decker, he asked, "What's the chap's name?"

"Ton Fish."

"Really? Ton Fish—from *the* Fish family?"

"Yes, sir."

"Mmm," Decker said, pausing several moments. I was nervous waiting for him to speak again. "I think it could work," he decided. I sighed in relief. "Be sure to check in at the office every morning for a message from my courier. Have a vague story ready for family and friends, something like needing to go upstate for a while to do some research for the *Journal*. In case we request Ton, tell him the same. He should talk of plans, vaguely, to take a trip West. Just know that when I send for you, you'll probably have to depart that day, perhaps the next morning. We want as much discretion as possible."

"Yes, sir."

Throughout the next couple of days, Ton and I were super anxious. But there was little we could do other than go about our regular business and wait. Finally, word arrived. The message read: *I need you both. Tomorrow morning, first sun—the Buccaneer.*

I went straight to Brown Bros. and found Ton poring over credit spreads or bond rates or something of the like. I placed the message on his desk. He read it and then jumped out of his chair and bear-hugged me again.

***

Early the next morning, we boarded the *Buccaneer*, a privately-owned sloop captained by a fella named John Bell. He explained our course. We were to sail out of New York Bay to the Atlantic and then head south, stopping first at the Florida Keys.

I'd never been on a sloop at sea. Besides a queasy stomach early on, which Ton found quite amusing, I handled it all right. We spent much of our time on deck, exercising or gazing out to the ocean. In the cabin we played cards, read, or just lazed about. Upon reaching the Florida Keys, Captain Bell showed us to a beach house owned by a friend of the *Journal*. Over dinner, he explained that he had family in Havana and visited there often. He had the proper papers for the dock authorities, and they knew he was coming. However, Ton and I couldn't be included on his guestlist because we'd have to later leave the island with him, which we weren't doing. The trick, then, was for Ton and me to avoid customs officials.

"I don't expect difficulty with this at the dock," Captain Bell said. "Lower-level officials there aren't usually overly thorough about checking the cabin. However, on the outside chance that an official decides to give our ship extra attention, I want you to hide behind the supplies in the storage cavern built into the ship's hull." Ton and I nodded.

Captain Bell continued, "While you're in there, me and the rest of the crew will disembark. An hour or so later, if the coast seems clear, a fellow named Carlos Carbonell will come aboard. He's a good man. He'll alert you of his presence by whistling softly, three times in succession. Then he'll guide you to a safehouse."

The next morning, we were back on the *Buccaneer*, ready to make the ninety-mile trip to Havana. The ride started out smoothly, but forty miles in, the waves began to roll higher, the wind whipped up, and soon rain started to fall. To ease my turning stomach, I went below deck and lay down.

The rough weather passed, and that night our sloop glided into a small dock on Havana Bay. By then Ton and I had, as instructed, taken cover in the hull's long and narrow storage shaft. We heard muffled voices, things being unloaded, and the sloop being tied up till everything went quiet for a stretch. We were scrunched in pretty tight, lying there still, quiet as can be.

Sure enough, after about an hour, we heard three soft whistles. We made our way out and found Carlos. Moving quietly under the cover of darkness, he led us to the ship's stern, then up to its deck, where we saw a rope hanging down to a dinghy. We slid down the rope and onto the boat before gently rowing toward a landing some 400 yards from the dock. Our biggest concern now was running into Spanish officials on the lookout for smuggling—whether by American merchants or by rebels. Nothing stirred, though, other than the water under our paddles.

Reaching the landing, Carlos led us on foot onto the side roads and back alleyways of a densely populated section of Havana. He seemed to know Havana's underbelly as well as I knew Manhattan's. We wound through dirt streets and alleys for the better part of two miles before Carlos stopped behind an unassuming, rather ramshackle two-story home, tightly packed among similar-looking homes.

We entered through the back alley. Inside we found two other men, one middle-aged, the other notably older, both armed. As Carlos led us past them to a narrow staircase leading to the second floor, they simply nodded without a word.

There were two bedrooms on the second floor. At Carlos's direction, we entered the one to our left and found two makeshift beds, a small desk, and a couple of wooden chairs.

"Here you stay," Carlos said.

"Thank you," Ton and I said quietly, not sure if we should be whispering or not.

"I go get Mr. Decker. He comes to talk with you. Okay?"

"Yes, sir," Ton said.

Carlos was about to leave when he hesitated, held up his hand, and said, "*Un momento.*"

Through the doorway we watched him cross the landing of the stair and knock on the door of the room across from us. A woman appeared, and he motioned her to our room. She stepped in the doorway, a little shyly, and smiled.

Our jaws dropped. It was Carmen Castilla, Evangelina's sister. We'd read about and seen pictures of her in the paper. And, my Lord, was she beautiful. She had soft, round brown eyes, long dark hair, a small, gentle nose, and a warm smile. With one look at her, I was a goner. My knees buckled. Never before or since has the first impression of a woman affected me so.

Though technically a free woman, Carmen was, to the Spanish, *persona non grata* in Havana. Yet it was in Havana that she could be close to Evangelina and her father, who'd been moved back to a prison in the capital. Therefore, it was where she wanted to be—even if she couldn't visit either of them.

"How do you do?" I asked, bowing, hat in hand.

"Good. And you?" Carmen said.

"Very well," I said.

"Nice to meet you. And thank you," she said to Ton and me. At that, she returned to her room.

"For now, we must stay quiet, you understand?" Carlos said.

"Yes, of course," Ton said.

"The family downstairs, it risks much. They do this for *Cuba Libre*, for women like Carmen and Evangelina, and for their own children."

"We understand, sir," Ton said.

After Carlos left, Ton looked at me, his eyes wide. "This is the most bully thing ever," he said excitedly yet trying to keep his voice hushed.

"Did you see her?" I asked.

Ton smiled. "She spun you around, young buck."

"I need to go talk to her."

"You need to focus."

Ton was right, of course, but, my, how I wanted to see Carmen, to learn more about her, to look into her velvety brown eyes, to let her know we'd protect her. It felt as if a magnet was pulling me toward her. I knew that it wouldn't be proper to visit her at this hour. Instead, Ton and I speculated in hushed tones about what lay ahead.

Less than an hour later, Decker knocked lightly on our door. He greeted us warmly but also with a sober air. We didn't need him to tell us how important every step was. He handed us a bag containing clothes fit for Cuban commoners, a pair of palm fiber hats, and two pistols.

"You won't need these till later," Decker said, "so leave them here for now. First, we need to spring Evangelina. We're doing that tonight."

Chapter 15

Decker explained that the Recogidas prison was about a mile away. He sat at the little desk in our room and took out a piece of paper to sketch the prison's layout and surrounding buildings. He circled the area of the prison in which Evangelina was being held. Continuing, he said that Ton and I were to be dropped off by way of carriage a couple of blocks away from the prison. We would be carrying a ladder, a plank of lumber, and two saws. From there we'd sneak along a back alleyway to a building adjacent to the prison. We would use the ladder to climb atop its twelve-foot roof, walk across the roof in a crouch, and then lay the plank from this adjacent building to the prison. Being at that height, he noted, we'd be clear of the nine-foot wall surrounding this part of the prison.

Upon walking across the plank to the Recogidas, we would be directly above Evangelina's holding area. We were to then crawl to the roof's nearest edge, reach over the side to a small, high-set square window, and, using our two finely-sharpened blades, cut through two wooden bars.

Evangelina was expecting us, Decker explained. "I've bribed a prison worker on the inside who has proven he can deliver messages discreetly. She should have already received word that we are coming tonight. She will know what to do."

Decker stressed, however, that perhaps the trickiest part would be getting Evangelina through the high-set window. If she could not find a way or the strength to pull herself up on her own, I was to squeeze through the sawed-off bars and boost her up. This is why Decker liked my height and slender frame. If we had to resort to this option, Ton would then have to pull Evangelina up to the roof on his own, then help me back up as well. This is why Decker had wanted a strong man.

If we made it that far, we were to re-cross the plank, head down the ladder, and stealthily make our way a quarter-mile or so down the back alleyway. I would then step out onto the street and light a cigar, helping Carlos spot me and signaling to him to pull up the carriage and whisk us away to the safe house. There we'd lie low until the following day, and the next trick would be getting the Castilla sisters, undetected by the Spanish, on a steamer bound for America.

When he finished explaining the plan in full, Decker asked if we had any questions.

"Might the other prisoners hear us?" Ton asked. Having kept up with the story in all the papers, he knew that Evangelina had cellmates in the new area of the prison to which she'd been moved. "What do we do if they cause any problems?"

"It's a risk," Decker said. "One that we've tried to guard against. Last week Evangelina faked a terrible toothache and managed to convince a prison doctor to give her laudanum. She often makes coffee at night for the handful of women who bunk with her. Tonight she has, according to plan, put a few drops of laudanum into each cup to make sure the women sleep deeply enough not to hear." He pulled out his pocket watch and looked at it. "We leave soon."

"All right," Ton said, looking my way. "You ready, old boy?"

I nodded.

***

We went over the plan again with Decker while we waited. About a half hour later, we made our way downstairs to the alleyway, which we walked down a little ways before sliding out to the road. A brougham pulled up with Carlos driving. Quickly, we stepped in. I saw a ladder, saws, and plywood inside. My heart beat fast.

About half-a-mile from the Recogidas, Carlos dropped us off. We walked a short distance in a nonchalant manner to the alleyway which led to the adjacent building to the back of the prison. In the alley, we crouched low, with our saws tucked into the waists of our pants, Ton holding the ladder and me the plywood. We stayed close to the back walls of the buildings. When we reached the one adjacent to the prison, Ton set the ladder in place, grabbed the plywood from me, and up we went.

Staying low, we moved along the roof of this adjacent building until we reached the edge at which Ton was to set the plywood. Before starting across, we peered over the edge of the roof and saw a guard pacing a little ways off. We edged back and took a deep breath, hoping this guard wouldn't glance up while we quickly tip-toed along the plywood to the prison roof. We made it across. Kneeling low, Ton pulled the plywood prison-side. Then we slunk along the prison roof to the building's northwest corner, near the small, high-set window with bars we aimed to saw open.

Lying on our sides, we reached over the edge, found the window's bars, and started sawing. We had to lean the sides of our bodies into the roof to try to gain leverage. Ton worked on one bar, me on another. Not long after we started, Evangelina, apparently standing on something, reached a small piece of white cloth up near the window opening. This was the sign that all was clear.

The sharp blades worked their way through the bars and, to my surprise, did so quietly. Still, I worried that we'd wake the other prisoners. It didn't help that, looking down, I could see Evangelina glancing anxiously over to her sleeping cellmates and then back up to us.

My nerves settled a bit once Ton and I had cut through the bottom portions of the bars without incident. We were about halfway through the top portions when we suddenly heard voices below. A black square of silken cloth briefly came into view. This was the predetermined signal that all was not clear.

Ton and I stopped and listened. The voices below continued. We waited, lying on our sides, for a few minutes. We couldn't make out the meaning, but we could hear muted voices still conversing. We weren't sure how to proceed.

A few minutes later, the talk quieted. We waited several minutes longer, hearts beating fast. The black cloth came into view again. At that point, we decided to abort the mission.

I stepped out onto the street and lit my cigar to signal the carriage. Decker pulled up. He was surprised to find that we did not have Evangelina with us. Once we explained, he sighed and said, "I'm afraid time is short. If she gives us the go-ahead through my intermediary, we will return tomorrow night. Let's just hope no one notices the compromised window bars."

***

Ton and I returned to the safehouse having been awake for nearly twenty-four hours. We went straight to sleep and didn't arise until the sun had run a good way across the sky. We'd been awake only a few minutes when we heard a soft knock on the door. I opened it and found Carmen standing before me. My heart jumped. I bowed again. *Stop bowing*, I thought to myself. *She probably thinks you're a little goofy, bowing all the time.*

"Coffee?" Carmen asked.

"Yes, *gracias*."

I motioned her in, and she placed two coffees on the desk. Ton picked up a cup and took a sip. "This is great. Thank you," he said.

Carmen flashed her beautiful smile. "Would you like some breakfast?"

"Yes," we both said at once. I felt famished. We hadn't eaten a proper meal in some time.

"One moment," she said, stepping away and heading downstairs.

"Wow," I said to Ton once she was out of earshot.

He smiled and shook his head. "Now's your chance, old boy."

Carmen returned with a plate of eggs and fruit.

"*Señorita* Perez made this," she said, motioning downstairs. Apparently, the Perez family were our hosts in this safehouse. I was moved by how much they were risking. "I hope you like it."

Carmen then turned to go back into her room. I wanted to stop her, only the words wouldn't come.

Ton whispered to me quickly, "See if she wants to join us."

I walked to Carmen's room and gently knocked at her door.

"Carmen," I said when she answered.

"Yes?"

"I was wondering, would you like to join us while we eat?"

She paused for a moment. Then she smiled. "Yes, *gracias*."

I brought a chair in from her room and during breakfast, we were able to ask Carmen about her life. Her mother had died when she was young. From then on, she said, she was raised by her father and older sister Evangelina. The three lived in relative happiness in Camiguey, with its winding alleyways, little shops, and rivers. She described what it was like when the revolution started and how her father first got arrested. She spoke of the peaceful rhythms in the Isle of Pines, the terror she felt on the night Evangelina was attacked, and the harshness of the Recogidas prison.

After breakfast, Ton got up and said he was going to sit out in the hall to write some letters. Really, he wanted to give Carmen and me time alone together.

She asked about my life. I told her that my father died when I was a boy, about how hard my mother worked, about being a newsie, and about Ton. She wanted to know what New York City looked like. America clearly represented something big and bold and hopeful to her.

For a couple of hours, the conversation flowed free and easy. Watching that shy smile of hers emerge while she'd try to find the right word in English to get her meaning across, or seeing her eyes widen as she listened to me tell her about streetcars and moving pictures and the hustle and bustle of Wall Street, was captivating. I know it might sound young and unrealistic, but I knew I'd fallen in love.

In the early afternoon, Decker arrived with word that Evangelina had given us the go-ahead. "We will try again tonight," he said. "Try to get some rest."

Ton fell asleep straight away, but as I lay down, I could think only of Carmen. Eventually, I got up and walked across the hall to her room to talk some more.

She got out some dominoes and while we played, she asked about our mission.

"Are you nervous?"

"A little bit," I said. "I think it'll go fine this time, though. Your sister is going to be all right."

Carmen reached out and touched my hand. Her touch rippled through every part of my being. "Thank you."

"Of course."

"I've enjoyed our time together," I said. "When we get to America, I would like to see you more often."

She looked at me with those deep brown eyes and nodded, and my heart soared again. I wanted to lean in for a kiss, but I thought it perhaps too soon to try.

Chapter 16

As we lay on the roof of the Recogidas for the second night in a row, I felt pretty confident. So far things had gone as planned: the drop off, the climb to the adjacent roof, getting across our plank to the prison roof. And Evangelina had waved her white handkerchief.

In short order, we finished sawing through the bars. When we did, Evangelina, who'd been discreetly tracking our progress, tried to reach up to us, only she couldn't get quite high enough, so I slipped through the window and dropped into her holding cell. Taking a quick look around, I saw women lying in bunks along the far wall, twenty feet or so away. They all appeared fast asleep. *The laudanum must've worked*, I figured.

I boosted Evangelina upward. Ton grabbed hold of her wrists and pulled her through. Next, he reached down for me. I jumped, and he managed to grab hold of my wrists. He started to pull me up, except I didn't have my hands turned the proper way and he didn't have a very good grip. So as he yanked, I slipped through his hands back to the floor with a thud. I looked beyond the bunks, out through a barred door, and saw a guard emerge at the cell door. I quickly jumped again, this time with my hands positioned better. I heard the guard holler and ring a cowbell just as Ton pulled me through.

"Let's go!" I urged, scrambling onto the roof. We hustled to the plank, laid it from roof-to-roof, swiftly tiptoed across, dashed to the ladder, and climbed down. We could hear the cowbell ringing and guards hollering. We sprinted down the back alleyway. When we'd covered enough ground, I pulled the cigar out of my pocket and lit it. Then I popped out onto the street. Luckily,

Decker had heard commotion and had pulled up to our rendezvous point. We piled in, Decker gave the horses a jolt, and off we flew. I looked through the back window of our carriage and saw another behind us. Two prison guards had jumped upon it and were snapping the reins.

"*Vamanos! Vamanos!*" Evangelina said.

Decker skillfully wound the carriage through turns and back roads, but the guards seemed to be gaining. We approached an intersection at a fast clip several blocks from our safehouse. Decker pulled out a red cloth and waved it. Up ahead, I saw that another carriage was about to cross the street. Were this carriage to do so, we'd collide. Thankfully, it waited. Right after we raced through the intersection, I looked back and saw it move forward a little before stopping in the middle of the intersection. Our pursuers had no choice but to stop. Decker smiled. "Perfect," he said.

Decker made a couple of turns and soon dropped us off at the safehouse and sped away. Inside, Ton and I led Evangelina upstairs to Carmen. They hugged each other tightly, crying tears of joy.

***

It took Ton and me a good while to settle our nerves that night.

"Now this is living, old boy," Ton kept saying as we tried to sleep.

We both knew our job wasn't done. We needed to help the Castilla sisters execute the final stroke of their escape—boarding an American steamer in broad daylight.

When we awoke late the next morning, Ton and I joined Evangelina and Carmen in their room for Cuban tortillas and fruit, which our host family had kindly brought up. We didn't say much as we ate. We all knew that getting this final part of the plan right could mean the difference between life and death. Both Evangelina and Carmen, with their beautiful smiles and warm eyes, did thank us for helping them. We said it was they who should be thanked for their courage.

Just after noon, rested and nourished, we put on our outfits for the getaway. Ton and I, wearing the clothes Decker had left for us, were dressed like ordinary Cubans. The pants, though, in case our escape went terribly awry, had holes in the pockets, which we could use to grab the pistols strapped to our thighs. The Castilla sisters, meanwhile, dressed as if they were Cuban teenage boys. They wore baggy slacks, oversized men's shirts, and boys' shoes. The key elements of their disguises were their over-sized hats, trimmed hair—greased to align smartly with their skulls—and their cigars.

Before leaving the safehouse, Ton and I showed them how to walk like boys. At first, they looked ridiculous, jaunting about, overdoing it. We rolled watching them, and Evangelina and Carmen had a good laugh, too. It was nice to see them smiling. As I say, both had been pretty quiet, as if a dark cloud hung over them, Carmen in particular. I hoped these moments of levity would brighten their spirits. But when we'd finished practicing and waited for the carriage, I realized that the cloud seeming to hang over Carmen had returned.

Upon spotting the carriage approach by way of the back alley, we slipped out of the house and alighted. Riding in silence, Decker maneuvered the carriage as close as he could to the docks before stopping to drop us off. Obispo Street was packed with shops and with people coming and going. As we'd hoped, the general bustle helped us blend in.

We had to walk about a quarter mile along Obispo to reach the entranceway of the quay. Ton and I stayed a half-step or so ahead of the Castillas, to make it look like a couple of older brothers were taking their younger brothers along to the docks. Carlos and Decker were following behind a good distance, armed as well. We tried to seem nonchalant, calm, and cool, but our hearts were thumping the whole way.

I looked out toward the quay, to the people walking on it along the bay, enjoying a relaxing, sunny day. I couldn't help but contrast their apparent ease with my tenseness. As we got closer to the guards manning the quay's entryway, I slid my hand through the hole in my pants pocket and rested it on the gun strapped to my thigh, just in case.

The trick was getting the sisters past the guards at the entryway of the quay which led to the steamer. Within steps of the guards, I felt a bead of sweat dripping down my forehead. I'd told myself not to look at the guards too closely, but I couldn't help shooting a glance their way as we came nearly abreast of them. I realized that they weren't paying close attention to the folks walking by. It was a lazy afternoon, after all, the kind that puts folks at ease. The guards barely glanced at us.

Once on the quay we walked a couple hundred yards to the steamer. Upon reaching it, a couple of Carlos's men helped us on board and an older man, the Captain, led us down into the cabin. Younger deck hands immediately went about undoing the steamer's rope-ties.

"Soon we will be on open waters, heading for America," the Captain said with a wink before going back up on deck.

Excited, I looked at Carmen. She, however, looked morose. There was the faint whisper of tears in her eyes. I was about to go over to her when she suddenly stood up.

"I must stay," she declared. We all stared at her. Turning toward Evangelina, she explained, "Papa needs me. If you were to stay, they would arrest you. But I am free. I need to stay."

I started to say something, to try to talk her out of it, but I knew in her voice that the decision had been made. Anything I said to the contrary would be futile. Evangelina knew it too. Tears streamed down her face. Carmen hugged her. Then she looked to Ton and said, "Thank you."

She turned to me next. I stepped to her.

"Thank you, Rory Mac," she said, putting her hand on my chest. I nodded and then took her by the hand. She leaned in and gave me a quick, but wonderful kiss. My knees buckled.

I helped her up the stairs and then, back on deck, I motioned to the captain to wait a moment as I helped her step off the boat. Before letting her go, I held onto her hand a few extra moments.

"Can I write to you?" I asked.

"I would like that," she said, flashing her soft, luminous smile. "Evangelina can tell you where to send letters."

I nodded.

"My father says he will die in Cuba and Cuba only," she added. "If he's released from prison, I don't know what might happen to him. He is old, and he needs me."

"I understand."

Watching her walk away, I thought about how much

I admired her. And I told myself that I would come back for her.

Chapter 17

Several days later, we breathed a sigh of relief as New York City came into view. And as we got closer, we saw a crowd numbering in the thousands awaiting Evangelina's arrival. The *Journal*, we'd later learn, had sent word throughout the city that Evangelina would be docking in Manhattan—while trumpeting, of course, its remarkable role in springing her from prison. Folks from all walks of life came out to see her set foot in America.

Her arrival, in fact, created an international sensation. The next morning's *Journal* declared her rescue "the greatest journalistic coup of this age"; and many agreed. Another headline proclaimed: "An American Newspaper Accomplishes in a Single Stroke What the Best Efforts of Diplomacy Failed Utterly to Bring About in Many Months."

When the crowd spotted Evangelina on the deck of the ship, it roared in approval. We knew Evangelina's heart ached, of course, for her father and for Carmen, but she was also elated. When she'd seen the Statue of Liberty for the first time, she'd knelt down and cried tears of joy. And when she stepped onto American soil, a jubilant scene erupted. Ton and I watched quietly, grateful for having played a part.

Folks marveled at Evangelina's beauty as she walked across the quay to one of Hearst's fine carriages. *You should see her sister*, I couldn't help thinking, smiling to myself. The carriage whisked her to a suite at the Waldorf Astoria where Hearst, always thinking theatrically, kept her holed up, allowing the public clamor and demand to build. Meanwhile, the *Journal* advertised the parade it planned to formally present Evangelina to the country the following morning.

Indeed, that next morning, thousands upon thousands came out to catch a glimpse of her on parade through the streets of Manhattan. At Madison Square Garden alone, the end point of the parade route, 75,000 were on hand to celebrate. The whole affair gave me hope that perhaps Evangelina's story had captivated the American people enough to make them more aware, and supportive, of the Cuban rebels' plight.

And, in fact, more American ink covered the death and disease occurring in Cuba's *reconcetrados*, the concentration camps that Spanish rulers had created. The purpose of these "camps," according to the Spanish, was to separate noncombatants from insurgents. In practice, at any given time, Cubans could be rounded up by Spanish officials and placed into these squalid, wretched places.

In the town of Artemisa, reports maintained, eight to ten Cubans were dying per day. On a single November day in Güines, some 600 people died on account of the horrid conditions. In Pinar del Rio, it was reported that children were using their bloody fingers to scratch into the ground to find small roots of sweet potatoes. Priests stationed in Cuba lamented that young country girls, desperate to survive, were turning to prostitution. About a month after we'd returned from Cuba with Evangelina, a headline in *The World* summed matters up: "Suffering Unsurpassed in Mediaeval Times."

I feared that Carmen would be forced into one of these camps. She'd taken refuge, as best we knew, in the home of an elderly man—one of her father's confidants—and there she planned to stay while waiting for her father's release. Evangelina said that her father was confident that Carmen would be safe there, and the home was close enough to her father's jail for her to visit, if allowed. Still, I worried about her.

Evangelina gave me the address to the house Carmen was staying in, and I wrote to her straight away. But it would take weeks for a letter to arrive, if at all. I wrote anyway. Carmen's letters, I'd learn, took even longer, only two of which ever made it to me.

I missed her desperately and felt trapped. If I went to Cuba, there was little doubt that I'd be found out quickly and imprisoned, perhaps killed. Officials would surely wonder what role I might've played in Evangelina's escape. So, instead, Carmen and I waited and wrote, hoping our letters would reach each other, that her father would be released, that Cuba would win its freedom, and that we would be reunited someday. Ton, of course, wanted to go to Cuba, too. He even went down to the *junta* offices to see if it'd be possible for them to smuggle him to Cuba with the Cuban Americans whom they'd been sneaking in to join the rebellion. They said it was too risky, that his nationality and acclaim would put the other soldiers at risk. So he waited, too, both of us worried that the attention Evangelina had brought to the cause was waning.

***

For the time being, we turned our attention to boxing. A week or so after Christmas, Ton declared me ready for a sanctioned bout. I'd fought a couple of unsanctioned bouts up to then—against guys that, I realized later, Ton knew I'd likely beat. But now I had a sanctioned fight against a young upstart, Louis Piazzo, a 5'9", 151-pound heavy hitter. I'd seen Piazzo fight at the Knickerbocker, and Ton and I both knew he presented a major challenge.

In the weeks leading up to the bout, we trained every day but Sunday. At 5:30 a.m., we'd hit the streets of Manhattan for a morning run, beginning at our old corner on Forty-ninth and Madison, heading to Forty-second, and then making our way to Bryant Park, where we'd do calisthenics, sit-ups, and pushups before crossing the lawn and picking up Sixth Avenue. At Thirty-ninth, we'd run over to the Union League for bag training, rope jumping, and ring work.

Outside of some early starters and the occasional shopkeeper clearing a sidewalk outside a store, we didn't see many folks out at that time of the morning. The streetlights hadn't come on yet either, so as we ran the morning darkness added to the quiet stillness of a city just waking up.

"This Piazzo," Ton said one morning at the Union League, "is no stiff. He moves, he's quick, he's powerful, and he's going to be hard to hit because he's so compact." He paused. "It won't be easy, but I've been doing some reading, and it seems to me that we can pull it off. But here's the key: I think you need to fight this bout as a southpaw."

"A lefty?"

"Yes, at least in the early rounds."

"I never thought about that."

"I'm not saying you can't beat him as a righty. I am saying, though, that I think we should think creatively. His trainer scouts just like us. They work hard. And I do worry that his strengths compare favorably to yours. My hunch is that he'll focus his defense on stopping your left jab, then pounce in close to attack your body. Everything for him will center on stopping your jab. So let's bring your jab from the other side. It'll mix him up." I nodded.

"We'll work at it day by day, but you'll get there," Ton said.

We kept at it over the coming weeks, and the training helped keep me from becoming overwhelmed thinking of Carmen. Still, each day Ton and I talked about the latest news out of Cuba, and much of it wasn't encouraging. In mid-January, 1898, for instance, hardline Spaniards rioted in Havana in opposition to the idea of giving Cuba autonomy. These hardliners even voiced their displeasure with the Spanish government's decision to replace the island's presiding general, "The Butcher" Weyler. General Blanco took his position. They considered him too soft.

The upshot of the riots, however, was that President McKinley ordered the *USS Maine* to port in Havana's harbor, so Americans on the island could be evacuated quickly if need be. It was an eyebrow-raising move, but the ship's arrival didn't signal that war between the United States and Spain was imminent. Outwardly, in fact, the Spanish government welcomed the *Maine*. Spanish authorities even hosted dinners in the capital for U.S. Naval officers stationed on it. Still, its presence heightened tensions, and this made me worry about Carmen even more. I wanted the United States to get involved so that I could sign up and go fight in Cuba. At the same time, I knew that this would mean the conflict had escalated, and Carmen was in more danger.

Chapter 18

As the Piazzo bout neared, Ton and I kept abreast of any developments in Cuba, even visiting the *junta* offices on occasion. There was, however, still little we could do for now, so I tried to turn my thoughts to boxing.

I'd started feeling more confident about our strategy for the Piazzo fight. The right-handed jab was becoming more powerful. Plus my left hand, from the relentless series of push-ups and pull-ups Ton had me doing, felt about as strong as my right. Rather than feeling sore when I woke up, by the last week or two of training my muscles felt loose, the morning runs felt easier, the bag work manageable.

It'd been four years since I'd first worked Ton's corner, and now I was the one stepping into McSorley's ring. The light shining down upon the canvas darkened the crowd, which was four or five deep all the way around, their faces further obscured by a smoky haze.

Piazzo and I met at the center of the ring. The referee broke down the basics: three-minute rounds, a minute's rest between each, scheduled for twelve-rounds.

"No low blows. Heed any warnings to avoid penalties," he told us.

Piazzo and I touched gloves and went back to our corners. Ton gave me a swig of my canteen.

"You fight at McSorley's, you drink Ton Fish water at McSorley's," he said, smiling.

I took a swig. Yeah, it still burned, all right.

"Now remember, work the jab early. Jab, jab, jab. He won't be ready for it. You hear me?"

"Yes."

The bell rang.

"Give 'em hell, Rory Mac," Ton said.

Early on, Piazzo's face told me that my lefty stance had him confused. Once or twice during the opening moments, he sneaked a glance back to his corner. I peppered a few jabs, two landed. Ton had anticipated correctly that Piazzo would try to move in close and attack my body. About a minute into the opening round, in fact, he made his first rush at my midsection. I fended off the blows effectively enough. But then, just as the referee stepped in to separate us from a hold, Piazzo fired a powerful blow just beneath my belly button, knocking all the air out of me. I gasped reflexively. Thankfully, with the referee separating us, I had a few seconds to gather myself.

I went back to the jab, making sure to move whenever it looked like Piazzo might be coming in again. He wasn't used to defending against the right-handed jab. I landed several in each of the first few rounds, and caught him with left hooks in combination a couple of times. Smelling his uncertainty made me more aggressive.

In round four, however, I overextended myself. I'd landed a couple of quick jabs and a hook, but Piazzo still forged forward. Eager to inflict more damage, I crouched down to waylay him with an uppercut. But before I could deliver the blow, he caught me with a power-punch to the ribs. I heard a crack. Then came a Piazzo uppercut square to my jaw. I'd opened myself up too much on the hook, just like Ton had warned, and had compounded that mistake by getting beat to the uppercut. Not till the count of four did I even realize I'd gone down.

I rose to one knee.

"Five. Six."

I widened my eyes, trying to clear the cobwebs.

Ton smacked the canvas: "Come on, Rory Mac.

Don't give in now. Get up!"

"Seven."

"Fight, Rory, get up!"

I popped up.

"Are you okay?" the ref asked.

"I'm good. I'm good."

For the next few rounds my survival instincts gelled with my training. I was careful not to overreach again, and I managed to fight through the fog. Exhausted, I jabbed and moved, jabbed and moved, occasionally offering a body blow. *Keep moving, keep fighting*, I told myself. I thought about Ton and our runs, about my mom and being hungry together, and I thought about Carmen and how I needed to see her again. And I fought.

"He's wounded too, Rory," Ton said, giving me a sip from my canteen before the start of the eighth round. "Keep working the jab and the body. Stay disciplined. He's wounded. I can see it in his legs. You're in better shape. He's going to break. When he does, pounce."

I took another swig.

Round eight saw both of us deliver tremendous punishment. Piazzo landed another powerful blow to my midsection, this time damaging my left-side ribs and sending me to a knee. I got back up quickly. Soon after, I landed a solid jab that made Piazzo buckle. Seeing my opportunity, I jabbed again, and then I went to the body before uncorking a left uppercut which caught Piazzo square on the jaw. Down he went.

I figured he'd find a way back up. He was tough. And, sure enough, by the count of six he was standing. At seven, the ref restarted matters, and for the rest of the round Piazzo was either on the move or grabbing and holding. I couldn't blame him. I tried to keep the pressure on, but he survived the round.

"Listen," Ton said, slapping my cheeks lightly. "Stick with the lefty stance for one more minute. Jab, jab, jab. Move, move, move. Listen for my signal. He'll be nice and spent and that's when you switch back to boxing righty. And then you attack, attack, attack! You hear me, old boy?"

I nodded.

Early in the next round, Piazzo rushed me again. I fended it off, realizing he had less behind him than before. And then I heard Ton whistle. I switched my stance and fired off a combination we'd rehearsed time and again: jab, jab, straight right, body, body, right uppercut. In my mind the sequence unfolded bit by bit, almost like time had slowed, yet I simultaneously sensed that I was moving sharply and forcefully. And this time, Piazzo went down for good.

Ton ran into the ring and picked me up. I held my fists up high and looked out at the crowd. Men were whistling and hooting and hollering. They appreciated how hard we'd both battled. I went over to Piazzo, and we slapped gloves and embraced.

***

To help me recover from the bout, Ton and a few of his buddies took me to the Union League. The energy and adrenaline of the bout had kept the pain from my cracked rib largely at bay, but now the aches and pains sharpened.

I took a hot bath and then sat in the Union's dressing room, rubbing chunks of ice on my swollen eyes and rib cage. Meanwhile, Ton and Pat and the rest of the crew were in the cigar lounge. By and by I got up and walked to the lounge. Ton and his buddies were sitting in plush leather chairs, puffing on Por Laranga cigars, sipping brandy.

When they saw me, the fellows raised their glasses. "To Rory Mac," they said.

"Wait, wait," Pat said. "We've got to get him some brandy."

He poured me a belt.

"To Rory Mac," Pat said again.

"The Survivor," Ton added.

"We ordered up a steak for you from the restaurant," Ton said. "You're staying here tonight, too, in one of the master suites. Your mom's been notified. It's all taken care of, Rory. You live like a king tonight."

I smiled and thanked them, and then I sunk into a plush leather chair, exhausted.

"Rest, Rory, till your food comes up," Ton said.

I did just that, sat back and closed my eyes, bone-tired and sore, while half-listening to their freewheeling conversation. They went from rehashing my fight to talking about finance to analyzing the situation in Cuba. I enjoyed just leaning back and listening, and the brandy helped the ribs a bit.

"We should've bounced de Lome a long time ago," one of 'em said, referring to the Spanish Minister of Cuba, who'd recently found himself in an imbroglio over a letter he'd sent to a prominent Spanish banker. In it, de Lome had called President McKinley a weak and low politician who catered to the rabble; when the letter was intercepted, it created quite an uproar in America. To a lot of Americans, the letter served as a window into the mind of Spanish authorities. Ton and I hoped it would reawaken American ire regarding what was happening in Cuba.

"I don't care so much about the letter as I do the *reconcentrados*," Ton said.

"Do you think we'll ever join in with the Cuban rebels?" Pat asked.

"I don't know," Ton said. "It seems like President McKinley is just waiting, hoping the Cubans somehow win on their own. But it's been three years and things are still nasty. Something's got to give. We should go in, put an end to this madness. Thousands upon thousands have died in those camps—and for what?"

"The whole thing's so doggone convoluted," Pat said. "I mean, shoot, today Rory's rag wrote that the only real question over the de Lome letter is whether *Spain* manipulated the brouhaha in order to start a fight with the U.S., in order to lure America in, so it's easier for Spain to explain to its people why it lost Cuba."

"It'll take more for McKinley to act," another said. "He's not about to go to war, especially if the folks holding Spanish-Cuban bonds have their say—too many ducats at stake."

"Yeah, but McKinley wasn't hired to protect Spanish-Cuban bondholders," Ton said. "Our government should be using its influence to protect the Cuban people, to help them become independent. Even Pulitzer's coming around to that, which should tell you something."

"Your man Schoenfeld says otherwise," Pat said.

"Who the hell is Schoenfeld?" one of 'em asked.

"He teaches history at Columbia and just got back from Cuba. Ton took one of his classes."

"Yes I did," said Ton. "And he's as bad now as he was then. I couldn't even follow his recent op-ed in *The World*. I mean, he admits that the Butcher's methods led to hundreds of thousands of Cuban deaths and that a couple hundred thousand more are penned up in the *recon-centrados*, but then he blames the rebels for it, says it's indefensible to rush off to rebellion, leaving your wife and kids behind. It's crazy. He compares the Butcher to Nero and then blames the rebels? Oh, he also said he thought Spain was going to win. I don't know about that, especially if we help the rebels more."

Sitting there, leaning back, this talk of Cuba turned my thoughts to Carmen—her beautiful eyes, her warm, reassuring smile, her strength. I pictured our reunion, and it made my ribs feel a lot better than any brandy could.

Soon, slabs of prime meat arrived, as well as cuts of fresh-baked trout and hot vegetables. To complete the meal, Ton ordered Neapolitan. We ate well, and then I slept deeply, in an immaculate room that, for all I knew, may have recently hosted a Belmont or an Astor. Winning fights had its perks, especially if Ton Fish was your friend. Still, my heart longed for Carmen, and all the perks in the world couldn't change that. Getting to Cuba could.

Chapter 19

Later that week, as I sat at a desk in the newsroom, the odds of the United States joining up with the rebels seemed even less likely. Spain had apologized to America for the de Lome letter, and now there was chatter of new trade talks.

The newsroom was generally quiet when all of the sudden a telegrapher picked his head up and said: "Holy shit!"

He whipped around in his chair and faced the center of the newsroom. All eyes were now focused on him. "The *Maine*'s been sunk," he declared. "It's a ball of fire. Brought down by a torpedo—or maybe a mine. Scores are dead."

"My God," an editor murmured. It felt as if everyone in the newsroom knew what this meant. War.

There were a few moments of silence before folks catapulted into action. Several journalists hovered over the wire. Artists began rendering images. Me and a couple of other cub reporters were sent to get reactions from the street, while other reporters were sent to elicit comments from Tammany's men, the Mayor's office, and business leaders at places like the Union League.

Out on the street, it was clear that word was spreading rapidly. People realized that everything about Cuba would be different now. The *USS Maine*, peaceably at port in Havana for several weeks, was at harbor bottom, swallowed whole, and 266 U.S. soldiers were dead. Folks were livid.

In the coming days, coverage of the incident was devoured. Hearst, naturally, worked hard to make sure the *Journal* provided the kind of in-depth coverage that

Americans wanted. He had already, of course, come around to the idea that the United States should be more actively helping the Cuban rebels. The *Maine* incident only strengthened this view.

As days passed and more reports rolled in, however, there remained some uncertainty about what exactly had happened to the *Maine*. President McKinley cautioned that the incident may have been an accident. He and others asked for time to investigate matters more fully.

My old employer, Pulitzer's *The World*, came up with the ingenious plan of hiring divers to examine the *Maine's* hull on the bottom of the sea floor, to determine with certainty what brought it down. Spain, however, wouldn't allow this. Further evidence, as I saw it, that Spain was behind it. Even if it wasn't, Spain had to answer for the *reconcentrados*.

I worried, though, that if an incident like the *Maine's* sinking didn't motivate the United States to help the rebels, nothing would. I mean, even the buttoned-down *Chicago Tribune,* for crying out loud, within a week and a half of the *Maine* going down, asserted that the time for conjecture as to whether there was to be war with Spain was over. "There is war now," it wrote. And yet McKinley refused to declare it.

Instead, he led the United States into a diplomatic game of high-seas poker with Spain that lasted two months, a gut-wrenching two months during which I heard nothing from Carmen. I wrote to Evangelina, who was now in Washington, D.C., to see if she'd heard anything. She hadn't, either.

Ton was baffled by President McKinley's inaction, too. Teddy Roosevelt spoke out in favor of aiding the Cuban rebels. To a lot of folks, the *Maine* laid bare the unacceptability of the status quo in Cuba, the chaos, the wretched conditions, the fact that perhaps ten percent of its population had perished—and a mere ninety miles from U.S. shores, no less. Spain had no business in Cuba, it was argued. And now an American ship—sent to evacuate Americans, if need be, and welcomed at harbor—sat at the bottom of the sea, two-thirds of its crew dead. To these folks the time for action had arrived.

The World, which, as I say, had initially played the war question down the middle, even came around to calling for U.S. action. It directed its angst over America's inaction at the business class, to which, it asserted, McKinley was beholden. At what point, *The World* wondered, did principle, our concern for our servicemen and the Cuban people, trump the business class's desire for certainty, for the status quo, for not rocking the economic boat?

In mid-March, about a month after the *Maine* went down, a respected war-averse politician, Vermont's Redfield Proctor, returned from a fact-finding trip to Cuba and reported to the Senate that the stories of suffering in Cuba were indeed true. Another war-averse senator, Nebraska's John Thurston, returned a couple of weeks later from a similar fact-finding trip. Addressing Congress, he said he'd expected to learn that the stories coming out of Cuba had been exaggerated. Instead, he came away feeling as if "an overstatement of the horrors of the situation was impossible." He talked about the shocking conditions that Cuban women and children faced, bringing tears to the eyes of Congressmen and to those in the packed galleries. By this time even "anti-imperialists," like William Jennings Bryan and Mark Twain, backed war.

Yet somehow McKinley continued to keep the United States from entering the fray. It's ironic, then, that history books came to characterize him as a plain old imperialist. I mean, I lived through it. The man moved like a sloth on this. Even the Spanish government seemed surprised by his restraint. Spain knew it was taking a hard line, but it feared a revolution at home if it were to lose Cuba, to appear weak, to seem as if it was caving to U.S. demands. Spain figured the positions it was taking would likely draw McKinley into war. Yet they hadn't.

Behind the scenes, though, President McKinley's administration was putting together the preliminary steps needed to raise a war effort. America had a startlingly small standing army; this meant that putting the country on war footing was a major undertaking.

Up till now, I'd put the question of my age aside. But in the wake of the *Maine*, the challenge of somehow joining the Army despite being just seventeen seized me. *How might I pull it off*, I wondered.

Ton soon provided a possible pathway. His family was privy to the behind-the-scenes moves that the McKinley administration was making in the event of war. One of these moves interested Ton greatly. We'd just finished a workout at the Union League when he brought it up.

"Have you heard anything at the *Journal* about what Teddy Roosevelt's up to?" he asked.

"No. What are you hearing?"

He looked around and lowered his voice. "Well, between us, word is McKinley's interested in raising a few volunteer regiments, mostly from the West, if war comes."

"Really?"

"McKinley needs men, skilled men. He figures a volunteer outfit of Westerners who can ride and shoot would be a big help. Roosevelt wants in, and he may be able to bring some Easterners along with him."

I hoped I knew where Ton was headed with this.

"I've already sent him a message requesting spots for us," Ton said, smiling. "It might just be our way to the front, old boy."

***

Ultimately, the war question came down to whether Spain would let Cuba go, free and clear, or whether it would demand—and Cuba would accept —an autonomy deal in which Cuba would at least technically remain under the auspices of Spain. The Cuban rebels, as you might guess, rejected plans for "autonomy," while Spain didn't want to grant Cuba complete freedom.

McKinley, still looking for a way out, focused on the three main conditions that he wanted from Spain: end re-concentration, accept an armistice through October 1, and recognize Cuban independence. The first was met only in piecemeal fashion. The other two were not achieved at all. In mid-April, then, McKinley finally asked for war powers. On April 25, 1898, Congress granted them. Eager to show that helping the rebels wasn't about imperialism, Congress also passed the Teller Amendment, which "disavowed any intention to exercise sovereignty over Cuba in favor of leaving its government to the Cuban people."

By now, Ton was convinced that the volunteer regiments would be raised, and that Teddy Roosevelt would lead one of them. He'd even had a talk with Teddy about the prospect of joining his regiment. This had a couple of big advantages. First, as I say, being seventeen meant

I was technically too young for the regular Army, but I figured I could more readily join the volunteers. Second, by joining up with Teddy Roosevelt, Ton and I figured we'd have a good chance of seeing direct action. And therefore, I could get closer to Carmen.

At work on the day the United States declared war, I saw Park Row fill up with thousands of onlookers who were on hand to watch the massive outdoor bulletins for any war-related news. At noon, when official word of the war declaration flashed on the wire boards, the crowd erupted with a roar. Many of the folks stayed in Park Row throughout the day and into the night, cheering as more reports rolled in, like that of Admiral Sampson saying that he'd meet any Spanish challenge with the thunder of his guns.

That afternoon I was sent to cover a speech by William Jennings Bryan, who was only two years removed from a bitter loss to McKinley in the 1896 presidential election. Twenty thousand people turned out for it, and they heard Bryan urge them to support McKinley's call for war. Speaking with fiery energy, he called on the onlookers to back restoring dignity to the Cuban people, to giving them a chance at freedom. He argued that humanity demanded that we act. He spoke about the responsibilities that neighbors share, and the support that friends should give. The man could give a speech.

Chapter 20

Seeing as the U.S. Army only totaled about 30,000 men when McKinley declared war, he called for 125,000 volunteers. Yet his military advisers still feared this wouldn't be enough, which prompted the unusual decision to establish three voluntary regiments, to be composed primarily of frontiersman, one of which became known as the Rough Riders.

While the bulk of the Rough Riders were indeed men from Western backgrounds, Teddy Roosevelt did have some other open spots in putting together the 1,000 men that would make up the regiment. As he'd told Ton, he planned to mix in about 50 "gentlemen rankers," men largely from the Ivy Leagues. Ton felt confident that we'd be included in that group.

I was awfully nervous, though. Competition for the "gentleman ranker" spots was fierce. Word in the newspapers was that for every applicant Teddy accepted, twenty or more would face rejection, even though only those who thought they had a shot—largely Ivy Leaguers—took the time to submit applications.

Waiting for the official word to come down on whether or not we were "in" was excruciating. I took solace in the Fish family's close ties with the Roosevelts. Teddy knew full well the power and influence of the Fishes, stretching back to Ham's great-grandfather—the one who served with distinction in the Revolutionary War, who played a big role in developing Manhattan, married a Stuyvesant, and was good friends with Alexander Hamilton. It also had to help, I imagined, that Ton had starred in crew at Columbia and gone west. Teddy, of course, also knew of the role Ton and I had played in springing Evangelina. But would this be enough for *me* to land a spot with the Rough Riders?

I received my answer a short time later, before one of our workouts at the Union League, when Ton greeted me with a big smile and said, "We're in, old boy."

My heart leapt. There were men all throughout Manhattan with way more money and influence than I who wanted this opportunity. But not many of them had Ton in their corner.

Ton told me of a few others he knew that made the cut, like Knickerbocker Woodbury Kane, a *bon vivant*, skilled yachtsman, big-game hunter, and former Harvard football player, known for his immaculate clothes. He even hunted game in South Africa and, legend held, had made more than one woman pass out from his looks. I don't make this stuff up.

Bill Tiffany, cousin to the Belmonts and grand-nephew of Commodore Perry, also made it. He had a fancy streak, evidenced by his reputation for changing clothes several times a day, which the New York papers liked to mention in their societal columns. His notoriety approached that of Ton's, particularly among the Manhattan elite. Society ladies loved his style, and yet the fellows accepted him as one of the boys.

I met with Hearst later in the day to tell him my news. James Creelman and Edward Marshall, both considerably senior to me, had already won the hotly contested designations to serve as the *Journal's* main embedded writers during the war, so I wasn't sure how Hearst would respond. He was delighted and said I could have my job back when I returned.

The hardest part was saying goodbye to my mom. We'd lived together, just us, in our little apartment for nearly a decade. On the day I was to leave, I reminded her not to worry and that I'd send her money.

"Don't worry about me, Rory," she said. "Just stay safe, you hear?"

"I'll do my best, Mama."

We hugged and then, with tears in her eyes, she took my hands into both of hers. "Your dad would be proud, Rory, you know that don't you? Oh, he would be proud. He came here with nothing. All he wanted was to make it so that his family could have something one day. That's all he cared about. If only he could see you now."

***

Ton and I had to head to D.C. first, for processing. There, we were introduced to the Army's penchant for making people hurry up and wait. One afternoon during our stay in the capital, still waiting on paperwork, Ton and I and a fellow named Basil Ricketts—a kind of world traveler who was also joining the Rough Riders— sat down for lunch at the Cosmos with the District At- torney, Henry E. Davis, and a friend of Davis. Davis had arranged for us to stay at the Annalostan Club while in D.C., and he loved that we were going to be joining the Rough Riders. Naturally, at lunch we got to talking about the war.

"Think it'll be difficult to root out the Spaniards?" Davis's friend asked.

"Can't say for sure," Ton said. "I just know it's high time somebody did something over there. It's time to stop the suffering. It's time to let the Cubans control their own destiny."

"Hear ye to that," Mr. Davis said.

"Victory may not come easily, but it'll come," Rick- etts said. "An Army officer told me just the other day that in his view about one out of every three volunteers that get sent to Cuba will make it out of there alive." He paused and then asked, "I wonder which one of us will be the one to not come back?"

"Don't be ridiculous," Davis said. "What with your hardy constitutions and strong spirits, you'll fend off any exotic diseases and scout out signs of danger in battle."

"Perhaps," Ricketts said.

"Listen, fellows, you're all coming back. And when you do, I'll have you all for dinner at the Cosmos. What do you say to that?"

"Sounds good to me," I said.

Stepping out onto the street, I spotted a boy who looked like what I must've when I was younger. He was skinny and looked a little tired, but he was hollering out the lead story in the *Extra Post* with gusto. As I reached into my pocket to buy a copy, his words registered with me: "Dewey wipes out Spanish fleet, read all about it! Dewey says 'We have met the enemy and they are ours.' See for yourselves!"

"Thanks," I said, handing him a nickel.

"Has it begun? How could Dewey win so quickly?" Davis wondered. "I don't see how it's possible."

"That's what it says right here," I told them.

"Let's go to the office of the *Post* right now," Davis said.

There we got the latest, as best as the newsmen knew it, and in the coming days we learned more: The war had indeed officially begun in the Philippines, where the Spanish were fending off yet another rebellion. There, Admiral George Dewey, who'd been ordered to sail out of China aboard the *USS Olympia* to Manilla Bay, had won a decisive battle against the Spanish in a mere six hours, losing only a single man. He'd destroyed the Spanish fleet entirely, alleviating American concerns about an attack from the Pacific; in so doing, he became a national sensation. It looked like the folks who said we could make quick work of the Spanish were on to something.

A few days later, Ton and I were summoned to Theodore Roosevelt's D.C. office. There were several others there when we arrived—former New York cops and a handful of sinewy, well-tanned plainsmen who looked like they'd have no problem lassoing a steer, in addition to "tenderfoot" Fifth Avenue boys. Soon, Roosevelt stepped out of his office and proceeded to shake everyone's hand.

"Have I met you before?" he asked me.

"At the Maher-Choynski affair, sir," I said, shaking his hand.

"Yes! A bully affair it was. And, even though it hasn't been advertised, I hear you've been to Cuba before."

"Yes, sir," I said, smiling.

"Even bullier."

***

Much to everyone's delight, within hours we stepped onto a Baltimore & Ohio rail car, bound for San Antonio, where we were to meet up with the Westerners in our unit for training.

That night we rolled across Maryland, into West Virginia, and eventually through Ohio, Indiana, and Illinois. In St. Louis, where we stopped for a change-over to the Southern Pacific, I was surprised to find hundreds of people waiting for us at the station, all hoping to get a glimpse of the better-known members of our party—guys like Ton, Woodbury Kane, and Bill Tiffany. The papers had, of course, been spilling a lot of ink covering Teddy and his boys, but this was unexpected. I wondered how they even knew what train we were on.

After three days of travel, we arrived in San Antonio. Ton and I, and a few others, Kane and Tiffany among them, stored our bags and gear at the Menger Hotel, which abutted the Alamo. Then we feasted on a breakfast of roast duck, omelets, and coffee at the hotel restaurant.

Tiffany was still wearing his society clothes, but at the end of the meal he held up his cup and said, "It's all off after this," meaning the time had come to give up a life of privilege for that of a soldier. He stepped over to the Menger's changing rooms and emerged wearing a rough blue-flannel shirt and a sombrero. Don't be too fooled, though: the outfit had been custom-made on Fifth Avenue.

With several hours remaining before we were expected to formally report, we walked across the cobblestone street in front of the hotel to the Alamo, which was smaller and more worn than I would've guessed. Maybe I'd imagined it as a massive fort because its legend loomed so large. Its limestone façade, though formidable, was discolored where it met the sidewalk and for several feet upward.

Stepping inside, we met the Alamo's caretaker, Captain McMasters. Before showing us around, he took a sorrowful look at the Alamo's rickety wooden floors and then upward to its smoky old stovepipe, which stretched to a high window where its exhaust was griming the limestone wall outside. He apologized for the Alamo's condition and spoke hopefully of plans to restore it, if the funding somehow materialized. Roaming through its courtyard, Ton and I talked about the men who'd died defending the Alamo.

In the afternoon, we made our way to the outskirts of the city, to the open fields of Riverside Park, where we would quarter for the next couple of weeks, first in the Exposition Hall, then outside in tents. Many soldiers had already arrived at "Camp Wood," as we took to calling it, and over the next few days more would roll in.

At the park, we stepped into a processing tent to sign our official two-year volunteer papers. Ton listed his age as twenty-four years and eleven months, his occupation as railroad man, and his place of birth as Berlin, Germany—his father had been stationed there as the Secretary of the United States Legation when Ton was born. I put down eighteen years and four months, which was of course a bald-faced lie, and under occupation researcher and journalist, New York City.

A recruiting and examination officer certified our papers. Based on what, though, I couldn't tell you. He also determined us mentally and physically fit for duty. For the mental assessment, perhaps he used mind-reading powers, because I barely said as much as boo to him, scared as I was to have lied about my age. As for the physical assessment, I guess the officer's methods pretty much involved sizing us up. Our papers also asked the officer to confirm that we were completely sober while enlisting. I almost joked that he should double-check Ton on that one, but I didn't think it was the right time.

As we walked through the old Exposition Hall for the first time, making our way to our assigned cots, the Westerners already at camp eyed us a little sideways. Through the newspapers, they'd heard all about the big-money Eastern dudes coming to town, and I reckoned they didn't quite know what to make of it. I didn't blame them. The coverage of Ton and the other elites had been decidedly mixed. Some journalists viewed the Eastern "dudes" reverently, others skeptically—it wasn't uncommon for the Fifth Avenue boys to get ribbed for being out-of-touch dandies, to be characterized as the "la-da-dah boys" or "Roosevelt's terrors." No matter; it didn't take long for the frontier-bred Rough Riders to figure out that we could all get along just fine, for the most part.

Some of the Westerners even went out of their way to make us feel welcome. Take Ed Culver. He bunked near us, and that first evening in the Exposition Hall, he came over to welcome Ton and me. He showed us around Camp Wood and let us know what to expect there. In short order, we became fast friends.

"Old Captain Wood likes to get going early, so figure on a 5:30 wakeup call," Culver told us. "You'll get about a half-hour 'til roll; after which we'll tend to the horses. Chow's at 6:30. Well, they tell me chow's at 6:30, anyhow. I ain't never owned a clock, and I don't intend to anytime soon."

Ton laughed at that. He loved the idea of getting rid of his pocket watch.

"Where are you from, old boy?" Ton asked.

"Grew up out on the Muskogee cattle ranges, in Indian Territory, Oklahoma. I'm part Cherokee."

"That so?"

"Sure is," Culver said. "Now after breakfast, it's on to mounted drill. They've got us learning our lines and doing all these coordinated maneuvers. We're getting there. Watch the dust. Them horses kick it up something fierce."

"How long is drill?" Ton asked.

"Maybe a couple of hours. Dinner's at 1:30. After dinner, we get to skirmishing with each other on the parade ground, while the horses rest. In the evening, you'll see, there's yet another roll call, and then we do about an hour of dress parade. Only it feels like several hours. I reckon it's easier on the range, especially compared to that darn dress-parade stuff. Can't figure that one out. Can you imagine doing all that twirling and turning while someone's trying to kill you? Don't see that happening. Anyway, supper is at about 7:00. The officers, they have night school, but the rest of us ain't got nothing after dinner but time for cards and five-cent beer till final assemblage at 8:30 and taps at 9:00."

"Sounds like a full day," Ton said.

We didn't sleep much that first night in San Antonio, excited as were. Mostly, I lay in my bunk looking at the Exposition Hall's ceiling, anxious, till the trumpets blared at 5:30, just as Culver had said they would. The day unfolded swiftly, with just about every minute filled one way or another. At suppertime, exhausted, a few of us were sent off to the nearby bar to pick up those five-cent beers Culver mentioned—and, being one of the youngest in camp, I was put on beer-run detail.

"We pay fifteen cents for one of these in Tempe," an Arizonan told me as we were buying the beer.

When we returned to camp, soldiers went to playing cards, some to playing instruments—fiddles, and banjos, even an accordion. The accordion player—from Arizona as well, though I can't remember his name—played awful well. It felt free and easy, sitting outside, drinking beer, listening to music, and playing cards. Our bodies were tired, and deep down we were all thinking about the war, but for a stretch we let our worries slip away.

Soon the accordion maestro from Arizona started in on a rendition of "The Sweet By-and- By." A couple of fiddlers joined in, and we all started singing, quiet-like at first, then louder:

There's a land that is fairer than day,
And by faith we can see it afar;
For the Father waits over the way
To prepare us a dwelling place there.

In the sweet (in the sweet)
By and by (by and by)
We shall meet on that beautiful shore;
In the sweet (in the sweet)
By and by (by and by)
We shall meet on that beautiful shore.

Chapter 21

We made for quite a cast of characters, that's for sure. I suppose that's why the newspapers took to writing about the Rough Riders so much. Technically, we were the First United States Volunteer Cavalry, but it was the papers that, early on, took to calling us the "Rough Riders." The name came from Buffalo Bill Cody's Wild West Show. I thought it was pretty catchy, although Teddy and Ton didn't like it at first. They thought it would keep Americans from taking our regiment seriously. They warmed up to it, though, as it took on a life of its own.

Teddy, of course, became the most famous Rough Rider of all. But even before he became the President of the United States, he was larger than life. He'd been a championship-level prizefighter, graduated from Harvard, authored many books, fathered six children, traveled the Badlands, and served as the police commissioner of New York City and the Assistant Secretary of the Navy, all before becoming a Rough Rider.

He was quirky, too. He would swim the Potomac naked for exercise, seemed literally indefatigable, had terrible eyesight—in fact, he had a special Rough Rider uniform designed with several pockets in which he could store extra bifocals in the event he lost a pair—and yet learned to be a crack shot hunter. Later, in 1912, he was shot while giving a speech during his independent presidential run and refused treatment until he'd finished his remarks. He nearly died again a short time later, this time from fever, hunger, and delirium during an expedition with a Brazilian explorer to map the previously uncharted Amazon River, which he went on after losing the election of 1912.

Within a fortnight of arriving in San Antonio with Colonel Wood, Teddy, a colossal ball of energy, made sure that our mounted lines and maneuvers looked sharp and our field skirmishes technically sound. Yet there's more to leading than task-mastering, and while Lieutenant Colonel Roosevelt worked us hard, he knew how to connect with soldiers in a particular way.

For all his energy and panache and bravado, he dealt with the men more leniently than Colonel Wood. At one point during camp, for example, he called a group of Rough Riders up to a bar outside a sally port and told them he appreciated how hard they'd been working. Then he opened a tab and gave them full rein.

When Colonel Wood learned that Roosevelt had plied a whole squadron with unlimited beer, he told a group of officers at dinner, in front of Teddy, that "an officer who would go out with a large batch of men and drink with them was quite unfit to hold a commission." The fellows just stared back in silence, knowing full well that he had aimed his remarks at Teddy. Roosevelt accepted the rebuke without comment and a short time later went to Colonel Wood's tent to apologize, saying, "I wish to say, sir, that I agree with what you said. I consider myself the damnedest ass within ten miles of this camp. Good night."

But that didn't keep Teddy from letting the "avenuers" wear Abercrombie shirts or allowing the cowboys to eschew their felt Army hats in favor of sombreros or their McClellan saddles in favor of the wider Mexican saddles they'd grown up on. And it didn't keep him, while strolling through camp, from giving guys who might've been playing an illegal game of cards a heads-up that Colonel Wood was coming.

In these early weeks, Teddy's promotions were about the only thing he did to cause some grumblings among the ranks. He put Woodbury Kane in charge of rapid-fire guns, for instance. Some folks didn't think this was warranted. In Teddy's view, though, Woodbury was someone he knew and could trust. They'd both gone to Harvard, they'd hunted together, and Teddy was impressed in San Antonio when he saw Woodbury attack kitchen duty with zeal, making a meal for some New Mexico Rough Riders as if they'd come to Delmonico's. Furthermore, to Teddy, it made sense to put Woodbury in charge of rapid-fire guns, seeing as it was Woodbury and Tiffany and a few other New Yorkers who had purchased the Colt automatics to begin with. These guns could fire 500 rounds a minute with accuracy up to 2,000 yards. In the end, Woodbury would earn his keep. And so would the guns.

In addition to Teddy, among the motley cast of characters were guys like "Bronco George" of Skull Valley, Arizona. He was considered the wildest rider in the West. Apparently, he'd tamed more than a thousand wild horses. Legend has it that when he heard about the call for troops, he got up from dinner, mounted one of those horses, and rode through the night, past Devil's Gate and Dead Man's Gulch, to the nearest recruiting station. It was also said that he'd already claimed the lives of five men—for stealing cattle, cheating at cards, being out of line with a woman, or the like.

Albuquerque's "Dead Shot" Jim Simpson, it was said, could put a rifle's bullet through a jackrabbit's eye at a distance of a thousand yards, while riding a wild stallion, no less. Word was that Colorado's "Lariat Ned" Perkins could rope steers from a greater distance than any other man in the Union. He joked once about bring-ing his rope with him to Cuba. He aimed to use it to "pull some of the Spaniards out of the parapets of Havana's fortifications," was how he put it.

And then there was William "Buckey" O'Neil, the first volunteer accepted into service by the U.S. Army for the Spanish-American War. Before helping to organize the Rough Riders, this dark-haired, thirty-eight-year-old Arizonan of Irish stock got his nickname on account of his penchant for "bucking the tiger" at Whiskey Row faro games. He'd also edited and published a newspaper, mined, worked in the railroad business, and had even gotten in a shootout with a pack of Canyon Diablo train robbers. He called Wyatt Earp a friend. Teddy Roosevelt absolutely loved him. He'd seen a lot and survived his fair share.

While Westerners made up the bulk of the Rough Riders, there were a number of characters among the "roll of honor of gilded youths," as the *San Antonio Light* took to characterizing the Fifth Avenue set. In addition to Ton, Kane, and Tiffany, who I've told you about, there was Dudley Dean, one of Harvard's all-time best quarter-backs, and Yale's Percival Gassett, a hot-shot polo player out of Boston whose grandfather was Commodore "Mad Jack" Percival.

David Goodrich was a recent Harvard graduate and a former crew standout in his own right. His father was a surgeon in the Union Army and, in 1870, founded the B.F. Goodrich rubber company, which David would one day run.

Now, as I say, most of the bluebloods fit in straight-away, but a few struggled, like William Tiffany. He'd been out to the open air of Montana in the early 1890s to recover from health issues, and he'd learned to ride and shoot then, but for whatever reason he needed a little more time than the other guys to adapt to San Antonio. He didn't like the lack of hot water in camp, for instance, and he didn't hide his contempt for how our rations tasted. A couple of days in, he also complained about not having a clean shirt. Eventually he was allowed to go find his washer-woman, but the fellows guyed him unmercifully for doing so.

As much as Ton and Woodbury and other bluebloods liked to rib Tiffany, they had a soft spot for him in their hearts. They could relate to his struggle to let go of the high life, and they saw him as well-intentioned.

Tiffany didn't get ribbed as much as Allsop Borrowe. At first, the fellows didn't pay much attention to Allsop disappearing for a stretch each day. Somehow he'd slip out of camp, whether at the start of a break or some other way, only to appear again an hour or two later as if by magic. Shortly enough, word broke that he was making daily trips to a hotel in town, where he'd been keeping his valet for shaves and baths. The valet soon found himself on a train headed east, and the fellows nearly put Allsop on that train, too.

***

The Army had expected us to arrive for training with some basic equipment and a horse. For most of us Easterners, though, that wasn't all that reasonable, so until a group of Army-ordered wild stallions arrived at camp, we had to rent local horses using a portion of our pay—which amounted to thirteen dollars a month, plus an allowance for clothes and an eighteen-cent food ration, not enough for Tiffany to feast on roast duck.

About five days into our training, our proper uniforms arrived. Putting on the gray, light-textured shirt and sombrero-patterned hat brought to bear the weight of what we were doing.

As did the arrival, a short time later, of our Krog-Jorgensens carbines. They were the most celebrated part of our gear, and their arrival set off a cascade of whooping and howling among the ranks. Even I knew that getting a modern carbine, as opposed to the ones that left a dark plume of smoke in the wake of each shot, increased your chances of remaining alive in war. Teddy and Colonel Wood had fought hard to make sure we got them, and the men appreciated it.

In addition to the carbine, eventually we were each issued a couple of revolvers and a machete, keeping the Cuban terrain in mind.

Our two-person canvas Army tents, which, when pitched, were four-foot by six-foot pyramid-like structures, arrived about a week into our training, too. This allowed us to move out of the Exposition Hall to Camp Wood's outdoor fields. While moving our gear out of the hall, a bittersweet Culver took a look around and said, "This floor wasn't all that bad, seeing as I hadn't slept in a house in six years."

With our gear squared away and with all the training, you might expect that we quickly became a model of strict military discipline. Only we didn't. Sure, the first day or two, guys wore their uniforms proper-like, but soon folks started showing up for roll wearing those Abercrombie and Fitch shirts and the like.

Plus, a lot of our guys just weren't that malleable. Watching the more serious soldiers try to handle a fellow like Bill Owens, a cowpuncher and miner, was comical. The fellows had taken to calling Owens "Smoke-'Em-

Up Bill" because on the way back to camp following a night of carousing in downtown San Antonio, he shot the lights out of a streetcar for no particular reason. "Smoke-'Em-Up" didn't know a thing about the nuances of military protocol, and he didn't give a hoot, either. If his hands were free, he'd salute anyone, from bugler to corporal to lieutenant, and he'd address 'em all alike, too, with a simple, "How are you, Captain?" no matter the rank. If his hands weren't free, he might very well not salute at all.

One day, Smoke-'Em-Up happened by an adjutant, a strict-minded fellow, whom he didn't salute. This adjutant stopped walking, puffed up, and hollered at Bill, "Present arms!" Smoke-'Em-Up stared at him, confused, apparently unsure of the meaning. The adjutant hollered again, "Present arms!" Only, he was so agitated he emphasized the "sent" more than the "pre-." Still baffled, Smoke-'Em-Up just looked at the adjutant. Finally, the man stepped closer to Bill and asked loudly, "Can't you pre-sent arms?" Smoke-'Em-Up, appearing more amused than ruffled, took his carbine off of his shoulder and handed it to the adjutant, saying, "Here, take her, Captain, but she is not loaded."

The area upon which we raised our tents was ringed with all sorts of trees—hackberry and pecan, cottonwood and sycamore—and it was cooler at night than in the hall. Most nights, provided it didn't look like rain was coming, Ton and I brought our sleeping bags outside our tents, onto firm, dry San Antonio ground. Before nodding off, we'd gaze up to the stars and talk about home or boxing, and oftentimes Carmen Castilla and Jane Witherspoon. Both of them drove us in different ways.

Culver often joined us in sleeping outside. He loved

to tell Ton and me wild stories about his life growing up on the edge of Indian territory, of hunting and trapping, of skirmishes with frontiersmen and Indians.

At twelve, Culver had to know how to survive on his own. He learned things like which plants could get you through a hungry evening and which ones could get you killed, and how far you can stray from a water source while hunting a rabbit or some other small game. And circumstances taught him to stretch game when he got hold of it. Eat the meat, sell the pelt. Treat the feet, dye the fur, and then find a traveler with money at the summer markets looking for a good-luck charm. In ways, Culver's life in and around the Muskogee cattle ranges reminded me of mine on the streets of Manhattan—tired and hungry, devising ways to sell the last papers in my bundle. What it took to survive seemed similar: guile and gumption, the ability to measure a man and to work hard.

He told us about his younger brothers and sisters, who he largely looked after, which is why he'd signed up for the Rough Riders—to send money back to them and to see if this experience could somehow position him to give them a brighter future.

As much as Ton and I enjoyed hearing about his life, he liked hearing about ours in New York City, too. Life there seemed as exotic to him as his life on the range did to us. His eyes would grow large as Ton described the lives of high society, the luxury, the waste, the splendor, the absurdity.

Much of our training could be summed up as hot, dusty, and generally disagreeable, so those nights of telling stories at camp in San Antonio, of just chewing the fat, were a nice diversion.

***

About the time we moved outside to our tents the wild horses arrived. There were thirty or so of them, and they seemed to embody the heat, dust, and fatigue of camp. Perhaps the greatest displays of horsemanship Ton and I ever witnessed occurred in San Antonio that day. Eschewing their McClellan saddles in favor of simply standing around the horses with their horsewhips, "Bronco" George, "Lariat" Ned, and a handful of others tamed those stallions as if they were conducting an orchestra.

Now, the stallions couldn't be fully broken in one session. Us horseless Easterners, who were assigned to the wild horses, were expected to finish the job. I named mine Hell's Kitchen. He had a mind of his own and threw me off a time or two, the obstinate beast.

Even the experienced Easterners had trouble with their Western broncos. They found them to be higher-strung than the horses back home. Some of the Easterners even resorted to paying "Bronco Bill" to take their horses for a watering down by the river and further breaking in. Bill had a knack for it. Somehow, the horses seemed considerably calmer by the time he returned with them. I didn't have an extra sawbuck, however, to put toward that kind of treatment.

I tried not to complain about my horse, since no one had a more difficult horse than Ton. I tell you, his horse—Ton named him Bull—was downright mean, surly, and stubborn. But day after day Ton worked with him, slow and easy-like. He'd talk to him while he brushed him, rub his head while they walked together, and laugh off Bull's inclination to buck, even though he threw Ton off a time or two. Sure enough, by the time camp broke and we set off for Tampa, Bull was treating Ton like an old dog treats his owner. He was no nicer to anyone else, mind you, but when it came to Ton, Bull seemed like a different horse. Ton even taught him a trick or two, like how to smile. I think Bull came to remind Ton of Charlie, the Skye terrier he grew up with.

Chapter 22

After long training days, you can bet that Rough Riders found their way downtown, where the saloons sold cold beer, tamales were hawked, street musicians played their fiddles, and beautiful women strolled about.

On one such night, near the end of camp, Ton, Culver, myself, and a handful of others, went to hang out at a downtown bar. We played faro and rehashed the funnier moments from camp, like Borrowe getting caught trying to keep that valet, or any number of scenes involving Tiffany. Then we slid into a nearby lounge that had a band playing cover songs, like "A Hot Time in the Old Town Tonight," a song that had become all the rage across America, particularly with the soldiers.

Couples filled the dance floor and before long, several of our crew, Ton and Woodbury included, were two-stepping with a group of ladies. These ladies, in sharply-cut Western-styled bustle dresses, found it cute that Ton and Woodbury and the other Easterners didn't know the two-step, which calls for a livelier bounce than similar steps in the East. These ladies, clearly enjoying themselves, decided to teach the fellows the Texas version. I sat watching, thoroughly entertained.

The fellows looked awkward at first. But, next thing I knew, Ton and Woodbury were attempting lifts. Meanwhile, the front man for the lounge band was singing:

There'll be girls for ev'ry body in that good, good old town,

For there's Miss Consola Davis an there's Miss Gondolia Brown;

And there's Miss Johanna Beasly, she am dressed

all in red,
  I just hugged her and I kissed her and to me then
she said:
  Please, oh please, oh, do not let me fall,
  You're all mine and I love you best of all,
  And you must be my man, or I'll have no man at all,
  There'll be a hot time in the old town tonight!

Looking back, it is nice to see the fellows laughing and carrying on, having a good time, especially knowing what several of them had in store.

After a couple of songs, we strolled along the streets of San Antonio to cool off, and I noticed something up ahead. A group of men were hunched over in a circle. As we got closer, it became clear that they were watching a dog fight. Realizing what was going on, Ton dashed toward the men and jumped into the circle to pull the dogs apart.

"What do you mudsills think you're doing here?" he demanded.

"Hey, what's this all about?" asked the ringleader, a gruff-looking fellow.

"This fight's over," Ton said plainly, scooping up the injured dog.

The men looked at Ton and then at the rest of us, sizing up matters. They made the right call in letting us go on our way with the two dogs.

Back at camp, we tied the healthier dog, which Ton named Hawthorne, to a tree while Ton took the wounded dog into our tent for bandaging. He named this one Hester.

That night we slept on our blanket-rolls under the Texas sky with Hester between us. As we lay there, gazing at the stars, we got to talking about all kinds of things. Ton told me that he'd heard Miss Witherspoon had gone to Sweden on a Mission. He told me about first meeting her, of their last night together. I could tell he still loved her. We talked about Carmen, too, and what we might face in Cuba.

Late into the night, Hester let out a particularly pain-ful-sounding whimper. "Think she'll pull through?" I asked.

"She'll be all right, old boy. She'll get better, and we'll find her a nice home."

Ton was right. It took a couple days for her to start walking again and to regain her appetite, but when she did, we sent word through a few locals that we had a dog in need of a family. That evening, a mom and dad with two young kids came to camp to take both Hawthorne and Hester home.

***

The next day, I found myself looking at a slightly rising field, mounted alongside Ton and bunch of other Rough Riders. This day's drill was open to the public, and hundreds of Texans were on hand to watch, their pic-nic blankets spread out on the ground, like spectators at a regatta. Teddy gave us the go-ahead, and we unleashed the pent-up power of our horses and rushed up the ridge. I went to hooting and hollering with the rest of the guys when, suddenly, that young girl I told you about scam-pered out in front of us. Thank God Ton scooped her up to safety.

And thank goodness orders soon arrived calling on us to pack up camp and head to Tampa, putting us that much closer to Cuba. Cheers rippled up and down the ranks as the word spread. Before long, the whole regiment was raising a mighty hoot, dancing around, and kicking up its heels.

That next morning, the three sections of our regiment that were under the direction of Wood mounted their horses and rode to the San Antonio Stockyards. In the afternoon, the four sections under Teddy's direction, of which Ton and I were a part, followed. Colonel Wood had commanded us to keep only the necessities that could fit into our blanket rolls, so a bunch of the wealthy Easterners had to ship boxes back home. Guys ribbed Tiffany for having to send back a bunch of swallow-tailed coats and low-cut vests, all of which he'd been advised against bringing in the first place.

At the stockyards we spent a good deal of time waiting around and in turn getting hungry. Waiting became a common theme in the coming weeks. Finally, we were directed to load our train. It took considerable effort to get our horses into the stock cars. Perhaps the horses knew that the five-day journey to Florida would leave them in virtual neglect. It seemed like only Ton had an easy time getting his stallion onboard. That horse would've gone anywhere for him.

Sleep proved elusive on the train's hard seats, but the guys were grateful that Teddy kept sending coffee back to us from his Pullman. And the crowds that met us at our stops kept our spirits up. Folks were really treating us like stars now; it was truly remarkable. They'd gather by the hundreds, sometimes the thousands, to see in person those whom they'd read so much about. As we'd walk through the crowd, folks would reach out and tap Teddy or Ton on the shoulder, as if to reassure themselves that the men were real.

A couple days into our journey, Ed Culver and Ton

decided to have fun with the crowd. Upon pulling up to a stop in Lafayette, Louisiana, a large number of folks greeted us as usual. Culver stepped out of a coach wearing a blue flannel shirt straight from Fifth Avenue. He had on a Manhattan-made hat, too, and walked with his chest out, his jaw firm. On his heels came Ton, dressed like a Western cowboy from Muskegon Territory. Next came Bronco Bill, only he'd put on Woodbury Kane's clothes. Behind Bronco Bill came a-sauntering Woodbury, lasso in hand, playing his part as if he belonged on Broadway. A young lady tapped me on the shoulder, leaned in, and asked quietly, "Where's Ton Fish?" I heard another ask a friend, "Can you see Woodbury?" All of the guys played it without breaking character till we'd returned to our coach and the train was pulling out of the station. Then we had a good hard laugh and had fun rating the imitations.

That night, the train rolled steadily along while sleep came only bit by bit. At one point, Teddy happened by the little row of seats that Ton, Culver, and I had settled in. He and a few other high-ranking officers had been given Pullman cars to ride in, but Teddy liked to come back and hang out in the regular coaches with the fellows. In fact, during our stop in Algiers, Teddy had decided to feed and groom the horses at the back of the train rather than join some of the other officers for a ride to New Orleans ahead of the regular troops. The men noticed things like this. Anyway, I think we were listening to one of Culver's wild Muskegon yarns when Teddy stopped by, looked at us with a glint in his eye, and asked quietly, "You want to meet the Crescent City as it should be met?"

"Sure," we said.

We got up and followed Teddy to the back of our rail car. He opened the rear door and stepped between our car and the one coupled behind it. Rather than continue into the next car, he grabbed hold of handlebars and climbed atop the train.

"What in the 'ell," Culver said to no one in particular, as we began to follow.

The train wasn't going too fast, so we only had to crouch down a little as we walked along the top of it a bit before we took a seat and let our legs dangle off the side. The fresh air felt good up there, and we had a nice view of New Orleans many miles ahead.

As we rolled along and the city slowly unfolded before our eyes, Teddy, a great conversationalist, was in an especially talkative mood. He casually went from quoting rates on Spanish bonds—which he took to mean Spain was running out of money—to assessing New York's baseball Giants, to talking about the importance of keeping a spirit of individual initiative among the ranks.

By and by we came upon the wide, dark, and gurgling Mississippi River.

"This is living," Teddy declared, gazing ahead.

"Sure is," I said.

We rolled this way alongside each other a little while longer, not saying much, looking outward, when Teddy unexpectedly turned to me and asked, "Who is she?"

"Who, sir?" I asked.

"I know when someone's missing a loved one," he said. I didn't know at the time that fourteen years prior he'd lost his wife and mother on the same day, a mere two days after the birth of his first daughter. He knew loss.

"Carmen Castilla," I said.

His brow raised a bit, and he gave the slightest of smiles. Other than Ton, Teddy was the first person I'd mentioned her to.

"I see now," he said.

And then we went back to looking at the Mississippi below and New Orleans beyond.

***

We were still sitting atop the train, the sun now just starting to color the houses and shops of New Orleans, when we rolled into the station. Yet again, even at this early hour, there were scores upon scores of people waiting to greet us.

As we crossed the gangway in our brown-duck uniforms, young girls in white dresses offered us posies. Continuing on, gentlemen well-wishers tipped their hats or patted us on the back, while beautiful Southern belles welcomed us with warm smiles. Refreshment stations had been set up, and several of the young ladies were offering free watermelon and beer. We were quite grateful for the Southern hospitality.

Fellows were excited to explore the city, but orders came down not to meander far from our rail cars. Colonel Wood was apparently worried about Bourbon Street, and he wanted to get to Tampa as soon as possible. But ultimately the railroad company ended up delaying us again, meaning that we wound up sitting around in the heat, hungry.

"I could be walking along Bourbon Street right now, with one of those Southern belles on my arm," Culver said. "Instead, I'm sitting here with you two." Not until nightfall did the departure call boom through the night air, summoning us to our coaches.

Two more days of bad food and stuffy air loomed, but at least we were moving again. And we continued to find ways to break up the monotony. At one stop, for instance, some of the frontiersmen showed us how quickly they could hunt down a wild razorback. It only took 'em about ninety minutes. Then we smoked it and ate like kings.

With New Orleans about a hundred miles behind us, a commotion arose that got guys talking. It involved a private who must've tracked down some absinthe in New Orleans or something, because he was making a lot of noise on our coach, chirping about a whole lot of nothing. Guys gave him looks but he didn't pick up the clues. It got so annoying that Teddy quit a round of faro and left our coach in favor of his Pullman, calling Ton and me up with him as he did.

Sitting down at a desk in his well-appointed car, Teddy looked at Ton and said, "Corporal Fish."

"Yes, sir."

"I brought you in here to deliver an order."

"Yes, sir?"

"I'd like you to go back to your coach and smash that out-of-line private in the nose. He's too fresh for this regiment."

"Would be happy to, sir," Ton said, smiling.

"Rory, if Ton runs into any problems, move in and crack him one, too."

"Of course, sir," I said.

"Won't be necessary, sir," Ton said.

We saluted and walked back to our stock car. Ton approached the private.

"Listen, we've had enough of your talking, you understand?" Ton said.

"Mind your own," the private said.

"Why don't you stand up and face me like a man?" Ton asked.

The man waved Ton off and, under his breath, directed a barb Ton's way. Ton grabbed him by the collar and stood him up. The men squared up. Crouching a bit, Ton pulled back his right shoulder, giving the impression that he intended to punch the private with a right. If the private knew better, though, he'd have figured Ton would come in with his left hand, the one that hadn't been maimed in that rail accident. Instead, he moved just as Ton expected, and before the private knew it, he was rocked by a power-packed left jab from Ton. The private never even saw it. We didn't hear from him anymore after that. In fact, once he'd slept and had sobered up, he apologized for acting out and admitted he had it coming, something Ton appreciated.

As Ton strolled back through the coach to tell Teddy that the order had been carried out, he met a round of cheers. "To the queen's taste, Ton, to the queen's taste," Woodbury said.

Chapter 23

Our first indications of Tampa were vast stretches of sand dotted with the rather dingy-looking shanties. We were rolling along on one of the railroad lines of business mogul Henry B. Plant, and soon we came upon Ybor City, several miles from our ultimate camp site. There the train stopped suddenly with no explanation. And we waited yet again. Roosevelt and Wood were livid. There'd been plenty of delays and poor communication from the railroads thus far, but getting this close to Port Tampa only to stop was the limit for Teddy. He spent a good part of the rest of the day hunting down a half-dozen railroad officials, laying into them something powerful.

Roosevelt and Wood were so fed up that rather than have us wait on the railroad, they had us ride our travel-weary, hungry horses the final miles to camp.

As we approached Port Tampa, Army officials directed us onward to what at first glance looked to be a marvelous campground smack-dab in front of the wondrous Tampa Bay Hotel, a majestic, quarter-mile-long hotel that Mr. Plant had spent two years and some $3 million building. Victorian and Moorish in style, it sat on 150 acres and featured a golf course, casino, bowling alley, card rooms, and a spa. Gazing at it atop our weary horses, and looking pretty worn ourselves, Culver declared, "Well, fellas, I can finally show you my home."

We all smiled at that. We were then guided beyond the Tampa Bay Hotel's luxurious grounds and fine architecture to a makeshift military camp in an adjacent, less-appealing field. There we found thousands of other U.S. soldiers already camped.

It took but a few minutes to realize that Tampa's rampant flies and stifling heat meant that we'd face conditions similar to those on the train. Well, those of us camping outdoors would. Some of the bluebloods took rooms in Plant's hotel.

When the rains started falling, in a day or so, I think most of us outside would've actually preferred the train. At least we looked the part of a Rough Rider now, with our scraggly beards, sun-leathered skin, and worn, brown canvas uniforms.

Compounding matters, no one seemed sure how many troops—among the thousands now stationed in Tampa—President McKinley would actually send to Cuba, or when. And yet we could see the transport ships out in Tampa Bay; ships that on a moment's notice could take us to Cuba, to Carmen. Instead, we drilled and waited and then drilled and waited some more. It was maddening.

Not surprisingly, the longer the Army had us camp in tight quarters on these damp Tampa fields, amid the swarming flies and mosquitoes and humidity, the more soldiers started coming down with fevers. In turn, nerves frayed; fellas became awful anxious. Ton and I tried to keep our composure, but it was very difficult to endure those conditions and wait while we wanted to be in Cuba fighting.

Cards, music, and cigars from Ybor were about all that made camp life endurable. That and during the day, if we had a break, we'd play a little football or stage a turtle race. Still, day by day our impatience grew.

By mid-June, still frying in the sun and slapping away flies, we heard the news that Spanish soldiers had conducted a successful raid at Guantanamo, catching

U.S. marines bathing, literally with their pants down. The newspapers spewed venomous ink at McKinley for not providing more manpower to back up these marines and for trying to wage a "kind-hearted" war.

Finally, on a hot afternoon out by our dog-tents, Ed Culver approached Ton and me in a hurry.

"Just heard word's come down," he said. "We're fittin' to go, at least some of us are."

"What do you mean some of us?" Ton asked.

"Eight of our twelve troops, word is, have been called to Cuba straightaway. The rest'll have to keep waiting it out in this 'ere forsaken place."

"Well, who's going?"

"Can't say for certain…heard my troop is in and a few others, but nothing seemed certain. No horses, if you can believe that."

"All that training and no mounts?" Ton asked.

"That's right. Well, except for a few of the officers."

"We're a cavalry regiment, for crying out loud," Ton said. "You say your troop is in?"

"So I hear," said Culver. He was in Troop L, advance guard.

"That makes sense, I suppose," Ton said, pausing a moment. "Let's go, Rory Mac," he said suddenly, grabbing me by the forearm.

We double-timed it to Teddy's hotel office.

"Yes?" Teddy asked, having heard Ton's knock.

"It's Ton, sir. And Rory Mac."

"Come in," Teddy said. He was sitting behind his desk.

"Sir, I heard orders have come down. That some of us have been directed to Cuba. Is that so?" Ton asked.

"My goodness, word travels fast. How'd you hear…

ah, it's no matter. They've asked for about 800 Rough Riders, so some will have to stay behind. It won't be easy choosing, I tell you."

"Sir," Ton said, nodding my way. "We want in. Please send our troop."

Teddy scanned his sheet for a moment and then looked up. His pained look told us that our troop hadn't been called.

"Is there a way, sir? Is there anything we…Can we join Capron's advance guard? I've heard they're to be sent."

"Please sir," I said unexpectedly.

Teddy sized us up. He brought his hand down on his desk and said, "You're the first ones to visit me since word of the pending orders broke." He smiled. "How you knew that Troop L's going is beyond me. Regardless, I don't see why you can't join it. I'll check with Captain Capron. If he's fine with it, it's a go."

"We won't let you down," Ton said.

We hustled back to camp, eager to assure Captain Capron that we'd do everything he needed us to do and more.

"If what you say is true, if Teddy makes the request, you're as good as in," Capron told us matter-of-factly. "I'd like to have you fellas along."

Sure enough, that night we were transferred to Capron's troop. Culver said of his fellow troopers, "They'll allow you all are aright. You see, we all in our squad grew up together from boys around Muskogee, Indian Territory, and on the cattle ranges we just naturally judge a man by his looks. You two'll pass muster."

After Culver introduced us to the rest of the troop, Capron announced that he was making Ton a sergeant from the get-go.

Ton said, "Boys, we must always stand together, no matter what comes."

The men had seen how hard Ton worked. It was clear they respected him.

***

By midnight that evening, all of the Rough Riders called to duty had rendezvoused with their troop, per orders, at the rail lines near the Tampa Bay Hotel. As a regiment, we'd been tasked with reaching our transport ship in Ybor channel. "Looks like we shoulda stayed there all along," Culver joked.

We expected a quick train ride. Instead, the next twenty-four hours were full of delays and general chaos. First, no train showed up to take us. After waiting hours and receiving no indication that a train was actually on its way, Teddy and a few other officers fanned out to get information. The rest of us tried to catch sleep on the ground alongside our baggage. Teddy returned about an hour later without much to report.

Three hours in, a night-shift hotel worker suggested we try a nearby track. We marched several hundred yards to it, waited three hours more, and still no train.

The Army had warned us that if we weren't on our transport ship by the morning it'd leave without us. Teddy seethed. We needed to find a way to the ship, and fast. A slow-moving train happened by right about then, heading in the opposite direction we wanted. Teddy didn't care. He called several of us over and we basically commandeered it. It took some convincing, but eventually the engineer agreed to ride us in reverse for the stretch to the Ybor Channel.

Before we got to rolling in reverse, Kane and Tiffany

and the rest of their artillery troop loaded the dynamite gun, 3500 pounds of dynamite, and our Colt machine gun onto the train.

Though in reverse, the train managed a decent pace. We even overcame a train of soldiers heading in the same direction on the track alongside ours. They must've been stuck for some time on their track before getting rolling again because we hadn't seen 'em pass by earlier. Teddy and Ton and I stood alongside each other on a flat car as we overtook it. By chance, as we rolled by, we saw a couple of rather thin, sick-looking soldiers and came to find out later that they were Jim Booth and Private Charles Johnson Post. Post was an up-and-coming illustrator who'd worked at *The World* when I'd first started selling papers there and who, decades later, would become known across the nation for his art and work with motion pictures. Though I didn't know it then, they were part of New York's Seventy-first Infantry, with which we'd share passage to Cuba—and which, within a couple of weeks, would reinforce us during a Spanish assault in Las Guasimas. I'm sure they were startled to see Teddy and Ton, two New York celebrities, standing on a flatbed rolling in reverse.

We arrived at the Port of Tampa to find thousands of soldiers milling around the quay, uncertain as to which ship they should board. No one seemed to be in charge. Me and a few others were sent off to drum up information, and Roosevelt and Wood set out to do the same. Working my way through soldiers, scanning the scene for someone with an air of superiority, I found a fellow holding papers.

"Any word on where the First U.S. Volunteer Cavalry should go?" I asked, rushing up to him.

"The Rough Riders, eh?" he said, ribbing me a little.

"If you must," I said, cracking a smile.

"Looks here like the *Yucatan*. Yeah, that's right, the *Yucatan*," he continued, pointing in its direction, "with the Seventy-first of New York and the Second Regular Infantry."

"Thank you, sir."

Racing through the crowded quay, headed for the *Yucatan*, I spotted both Roosevelt and Wood. I called them over:

"The *Yucatan*. We're to head over on the *Yucatan* with the Seventy-first and Second Regular."

I thought Teddy would smile with delight upon hearing this. Instead, he shook his head and fumed, "Those lummoxes. No way can the *Yucatan* hold all of us. They're mad."

Originally built by the New York and Cuba Steam Navigation Company for transporting freight, the *Yucatan* was a 342-foot-long, 43-foot-wide iron-laden power-house, with schooner-rigging and three 300 horsepower engines, along with six massive Scotch boilers. It was impressive. But it couldn't hold us all. Thankfully, Teddy Roosevelt had been the Assistant Secretary of the Navy and realized this right away.

"Colonel Wood," Teddy said, focused and firm. "We must get the men moving and now. We need to get on that ship before it fills."

Within a minute, all the Rough Riders were marching double-time across the quay, with our mission-bound, bull moose leader out in front, aiming to make it to our ship before the other regiments. And we did, just in the nick of time.

As we piled on, Teddy made certain that a good

number of us stood guard on the dock to discourage other regiments from trying to force their way on. And when the Seventy-first of New York eventually made it to our part of the quay, Ton and Woodbury and several others stepped forward to make it clear that they'd been beaten to the vessel. Teddy declared triumphantly, to no one in particular, "A shade less ready than we were in the matter of individual initiative."

We sailed after nightfall out into the channel, where we dropped anchor and waited for the rest of the convoy to get in position. When it came time to sleep, we climbed onto bunks in the *Yucatan*'s cavernous hold. The bunks were built close together and made of rough wood.

"I suppose the floor would beat this 'ere bunk," Culver said.

"I've slept on better benches in Manhattan," I said, after turning over and catching a splinter.

"I reckon you can show this old cowboy around the big city one day, huh, Rory Mac?"

"You bet."

Suddenly there was a crash.

"Hot damn!" Ton hollered. The bunk board he was lying upon had suddenly given way, and he'd fallen to the floor.

"This here's soldierin'," he said as he got up gingerly.

Throughout the night, more bunk boards gave way. I'd be trying to sleep and all of a sudden *Boom!*, a Rough Rider would hit the ground. The first few startled me; the next few, I barely opened an eye.

Now, that first night on the *Yucatan* I was rather excited, figuring that we'd be bound for Cuba the next day, putting me that much closer to Carmen. So you can imagine the frustration when we spent all of the next day in that channel—and the next, and the next, and the next. I'm not kidding; we spent four full days in that channel waiting for orders to head to Cuba, sleeping in those shoddy bunks, breathing in the heavy, hot, uncirculated air of the *Yucatan*'s bowels. Compounding matters, the "fresh canned beef" they gave us lacked salt and tended to nauseate folks.

Space was tight and the heat was scorching, but being on deck was much better than being in the bowels. To pass time, we drilled and read Army manuals. And each morning and evening we hopped over the side of the *Yucatan* for a swim and to bathe in the Gulf's cool waters. This was the best part of our days in the channel.

Though we didn't learn this till later, our four-day delay was caused mainly by a false alarm. Apparently, a sailor, on a ship well ahead of ours, thought he'd spotted a Spanish fleet ahead, readying to attack. As a result, this sailor's ship, and a group of others, turned back to Tampa and basically forced the Navy to halt all ship movement until the path was deemed clear.

Finally, on June 13th, the "clink, clink, clink" of the anchor rising woke me up.

"Ed, Ton, I think we're gonna start moving soon," I whispered.

Ed stirred a little, turned toward me, and said, "'bout damn time." Then he fell back asleep.

Ton and I scampered up to the deck. About fifteen minutes later, Reveille brought up the rest of the Rough Riders. Folks were so excited that for the next couple of hours spontaneous cheers erupted on deck. Flags were unfurled off the stern, and the Rough Rider band started playing. Before noon, we were sailing.

The *Yucatan* was among a group of thirty-four transport vessels that, together in three powerful lines, crossed the Gulf of Mexico, escorted by the battleship *Indiana* and several auxiliary ships. Over several days, we moved methodically southward along the Florida coast, then through the waters of the West Indies. On deck, where warm breezes often brushed by, we passed time by staring at the blue sea and telling stories, tales of riches gained and lost, of love won and lost.

Colonel Wood worried that too much sitting around would make us frail and susceptible to disease, so for about an hour and a half each day, we'd hop around the deck in lockstep, holding onto each other's shoulders, working our legs and lungs. And we carried out daily training on how to use and care for our Krag-Jorgensons. Oh, and naturally, we played a lot of poker and faro.

We weren't sure of our final destination. Some guys figured we were bound to make landfall near Santiago, others Puerto Rico. I wanted Havana because that's where I figured Carmen was. On our sixth day at sea, Buckey O'Neil, looking through a spotting scope, sighted Cuban land. "There she is, there she is," Buckey said, handing the binoculars to Ton. Word spread across the ship deck quickly and cheers went up all around. Santiago it'd be.

Chapter 24

The next afternoon we loaded onto skiffs and rowed to a pier near Daiquiri, a tiny Cuban village. Ton, Culver, and I were together with other members of our troop, and it was Ton, fittingly, who did the bulk of the rowing. The channel's waters were pretty rough; it wasn't easy pulling.

Because the waves rolled so powerfully here, we couldn't beach our skiffs. Instead, the Army had tasked us with using the pier at Daiquiri to get ashore. But what the Army didn't seem to understand was that getting close to the pier presented a mighty challenge, too. To boot, the Spanish had torn off the pier's top-layer planks, meaning even after reaching the pier and disembarking it'd be quite difficult to traverse the pier amidst the rocky sea and make landfall.

Thanks to Ton, we were able to get our skiff relatively close to the pier without crashing into it. Then we jumped in the water and grabbed the pier's slick under-girding for support. Hanging onto the slippery boards, which were barely peeking out of the rough waters, we struggled to keep our footing as we worked toward the shore, half walking, half swimming, grasping for boards with our hands, feeling for rocks with our feet.

It was a precarious situation. I looked back and saw Tiffany lose his grip. The current quickly pulled him away from us. Ton and I, aware that he basically couldn't swim, went for him. Ton shot out ahead of me and was about to grab Tiffany when Buckey O'Neil suddenly popped up from underneath the water and held Tiffany up. He'd jumped from the pier and streaked underwater straight for Tiffany and beat all of us there. "The man lives in a desert and swims like a fish. Reckon that," Culver said, smiling as he struggled to hold on to the mooring.

Upon reaching shore, we hung our stuff up to dry. The rest of the day, those of us who were strong swimmers, guys like Teddy, Buckey O'Neill, Charles Knoblauch, and Ton, of course, fished out soldiers who got swept away from the pier or simply battered by the rough water and rocks. And it wasn't just fellow Rough Riders that we helped. The Army's Tenth Cavalry, a black regiment that would save our hind in a couple of days, as well as a couple of other regiments, faced the same precarious conditions.

If we weren't helping soldiers to shore, we were retrieving revolvers and other gear that soldiers had dropped while holding onto the pier's undergirding. So, as you might imagine, at day's end we were wiped out.

In hindsight, it made little sense for the generals to have ordered us to land at that spot, near a busted-up pier, in tough, rocky surf. Teddy was irate. Anyone with any sense could see the danger.

Sadly, not everyone made it. Two members of the Tenth Calvary lost their footing and got swept away out to sea so quickly no one could reach them. O'Neil and Knoblauch, who were the closest of our group to the two when it happened, tried to rescue them, but there was no chance. In a matter of seconds they'd sunk under the water and were gone.

We spent our first evening in Cuba setting up our dog-tents on a stretch of high grass not far from shore, starting fires and cooking up the putrid-smelling meat that we'd been rationed. Daiquiri was a beautiful, sparsely populated town in a river valley with hills on either side. Every now and again, two or three of its inhabitants came by to welcome us. They were friendly and seemed to side with the rebels.

With dinner cooking and camp set up, we had some time to kill. A group of fellows captured tarantulas and other exotic bugs and Burr McIntosh, an employee of the *Journal* who was embedded with us, proposed we race them. So we did. I matted down a grassy starting point and, using rocks, laid out a few lanes for the tarantulas to race along. We gathered around and soon the buggers were off and racing. I had a quarter riding on Culver's, but about halfway into the race those obstinate spiders slowed down and broke off their route. McIntosh reached down with both hands to set a couple straight and promptly discovered that racing tarantulas is more dangerous than racing turtles. He suffered several bites.

"Hot damn!" McIntosh hollered, jumping up and down, holding his hands between his knees. He eyed a shovel, grabbed it, and smashed those tarantulas.

"That's fittin' to keep smartin' Burr," Culver said, chuckling a little.

"I'd say."

"I think a little Old 'O' will keep it from smarting too much," Ton said to McIntosh.

"You got any?"

"Nope. Maybe another regiment will, or some of these locals."

"Let's send out a huntin' party," Culver suggested.

As such, Ton, Culver, and I volunteered for our first mission on Cuban soil, to find whiskey. We soon learned, however, that the other regiments didn't have any. Undeterred, we walked along a little roadway until we came upon a quaint store. It was closed but we made our way in through a side window and, while we didn't find Old "O," we did find some powerful Jamaican rum and sweet Spanish wine. We grabbed a few bottles and left some money on a table. We gave McIntosh first dibs. Then the salve was passed around as if everybody had been bitten by a tarantula.

For the next hour or two we sat by our fires chewing on grub, sipping rum, and letting our minds rest. As I say, we were nestled between hills in a picturesque valley which ran along the Daiquiri River. The peace and beauty of the night was surreal, knowing that war loomed.

By and by, Edwin Marshall, who, like McIntosh, worked for the *Journal*, joined us. Though we weren't talking all that much, there was a powerful, quiet energy rippling among us. The gravity of what we would soon face was setting in.

"Sixteen thousand troops, gear and batteries, and twenty or so horses in those conditions—and all in twelve hours?" Marshall said, shaking his head, impressed by the feat of our landing.

"When you put it like that, I guess it sounds like something," Culver said.

"Sure helped that the Spanish soldiers weren't around," Woodbury added.

"I suppose Sampson and Shafter deserve a share of the credit, you know, for making the Spanish think we'd land elsewhere," Marshall said. We nodded in agreement at that. We hadn't landed in an ideal spot, but at least the rear admiral and general in charge of the mission had put us down in an area that was free of Spaniards.

We sat there a while longer, watching the fire, looking out to the nearby hills, gazing up at the star-filled sky, making light talk till the night got deep. Then we settled in under our blankets. I fell asleep with Carmen on my mind.

***

As the sun's first rays rose over the hill east of us and shone through slits in our dog tents, I woke up. Ton arose a few minutes later.

"What in the world was in that wretched brew?" he asked, lying under his blanket, rubbing his forehead.

"My head's pounding, too. Feels like I just got done fighting Piazzo," I said, sitting up in our canvas tent. I took a look outside. Thick dew blanketed the lush foliage that surrounded us and ran up the hills on either side.

"I'll get that coffee going, for sure," Ton said. He laid a bunch of the beans out on a nearby stone and we used our rifle butts to smash them up. That's how you grind coffee during war.

Sipping dark coffee, Ton, Woodbury, Tiffany, Culver, and I cussed the wine and Jamaican rum from the night before and speculated on our next move. Our orders hadn't yet arrived, but we figured we'd be sent over the hills in front of us and to our west. Sure enough, we soon learned that we were to march to a village eight miles away, Siboney, which would put us closer to Santiago, the ultimate goal.

On the march to Siboney we stayed alert but encountered no Spanish. The only battles we fought were with the bugs and the heat. We had to hack through stretches of thick jungle and we each had plenty of supplies and ammo weighing us down, so it was slow going. But it was especially slow because of the artillery guns, which Woodbury's troop, earning its keep, worked hard at powering along our trail.

With darkness setting in, we set up camp on the

edge of town. While Ton and I were putting up our tent, a few native islanders walked toward us cautiously, gesturing and holding out large, rich green, royal palm leaves. It took a little while to understand their meaning, but we eventually realized that they were suggesting we use the leaves as thatched roofing for our tents, in the event of rain or heavy winds. It was a kind gesture and another sign of Cubans' support for the rebels. And these locals must've had some special insight, because that night a strong storm rolled in.

Ton and I were under our blankets looking for shut-eye when the torrential downpour arrived. Our tents, even with the thatched roofing, were no match for the rainwater, let alone the various jungle bugs and land crabs crawling about.

"You sleeping, old boy?" Ton asked after we'd lain down for an hour or so.

"Nope."

"Me neither. What d'ye say we put some ponchos over the rations. I'm worried they'll go bad."

"All right."

We got up, ventured out into the rain, and found Culver standing under a tree, watching the storm. He joined us in securing the rations, and then we took cover back beneath the tree.

"This is soldierin'," Ton said.

When the rain finally stopped, we started a sizable fire. As the flames rose, we stood near them with our palms out to take in the heat. By and by, Lt. Col. Roosevelt and Captain Capron came up, on one of their middle-of-the-night walks through camp, making sure all was squared away.

"You fellows dry yet?" Roosevelt asked with a wry

smile. You could tell he loved being up and about at this hour.

"Getting there, sir," Culver said.

Both men stopped to watch the flames with us for a bit.

"You all think we'll see live action tomorrow?" Ton asked.

"I should say so," Teddy said matter-of-factly.

By the flickering light of our fire, Teddy took in the scene. A kind of unspoken tension hung in the air and yet so too did a kind of post-storm quiet. In his memoirs published a few years later, Teddy would recall the scene. Of Ton and Captain Capron, he wrote, "Their frames seemed of steel, to withstand all fatigue; they were flushed with health; in their eyes shone high resolve and fiery desire."

Before long, Teddy and Capron moved along. Ton, Culver, and I stayed by the fire a bit longer.

"Both your mother and father still living, Ed?" Ton asked.

"Sure are, out in Indian territory with a sister and my three brothers—leastwise if one of 'em hasn't enlisted since I left."

"I suppose the people at home are thinkin' about us now," Ton said.

After a bit we tried to sleep again, but it still didn't come. I must've been rolling around, keeping Ton up, because at one point he asked, "You all right, old boy?"

"Yeah," I said unconvincingly.

"What are you chewing on?"

"Ah, nothing," I sighed.

"Don't worry, Rory Mac. You're a survivor. I've got your back, anyhow. We're gonna find Carmen. You hear me?"

"You ain't worried, Ton?"

"It's like Hawthorne says, 'Mankind are earthen jugs with spirits in them.' I figure this jug's already raised its fair share of hay. It's time to either win glory on the battlefield or die trying."

Chapter 25

About half past three in the morning, first call yanked me out of a short stretch of sleep. An hour or so later, our marching orders arrived. We were to follow a three-mile trail to the town of Las Guasimas, from which we'd be in a better position to attack Santiago.

At breakfast, Culver brought some hardtack to our fire. "I'm trying something new, fellas," he said. "Fittin' to fry this here hardtack, what d'ye say?"

"How about it. Throw mine on if you don't mind," I said.

Ton took Culver up on it, too.

"What do you say to more tomatoes, Ton?" one of the soldiers in our troop, Joseph, asked. "They'll go nicely with Culver's fried tack."

"How many tomatoes have we got left?" Ton asked.

"Several cans," Culver said, checking.

"Well, let's open 'em up. We're liable to all be killed today; we may as well have enough to eat," Ton said, eerily.

It was a darn good breakfast considering, but I hated when Ton talked that way. He spoke ominously again a short time later, as we were packing our stuff. He'd chucked aside an extra pair of shoes when Culver said, "You might want to hold onto those. They could come in handy." Culver wasn't one to just disregard a seven-dollar pair of shoes.

"Nah, I don't think I'll need them anymore," Ton said.

As advance scouts, our troop gathered at the front of the Rough Rider regiment, along a narrow pathway with thick bushes and prickly cactus on either side. Our supply guys managed to get the rear mule trains and mess kits loaded up, and we were anxious to get going, but we needed to await a final order. After about thirty minutes with no word, we took off our heavy gear and lay down. The Army was again showing us its particular ability to make people wait. Even Colonel Wood, tired and hoarse, grew impatient. Teddy seemed unfazed, though. He stayed in constant motion, going up and down the pathway, checking on guys' spirits, encouraging them, spreading his energy around.

Finally, we were ordered onward. The first stretch of the three-mile journey, led by Captain Capron and Ton, included steep, rolling hills that were several hundred feet high. Guided by a local Cuban, we moved up and over the hills at a relatively quick pace. The sun was already quite potent and, with our camp equipment and weapons, including our 200 rounds of ammo per person, it was a pretty challenging hike.

We stopped briefly several times to rest as we ascended the bigger hills. Most of the Rough Riders, of course, were plains cowboys who hadn't done much hiking, and we'd done a lot of our training on horseback. So this wasn't easy, and as the day wore on, it got hotter and hotter under the relentless sun. Still, we carried on; well, most of us, at least. Some guys just couldn't take the heat and the pace, so they dropped out of line, utterly exhausted.

Upon reaching a summit among this batch of hills, we took another break. I looked down and back, to the impressive sight of the bay and the sun-drenched villages. I saw the tent-camps of the regiments behind us and I heard occasional bugle calls rising softly. If not for the fact that war loomed, it'd have made for a lovely scene.

An easier, flatter stretch across jungle-like terrain ensued. During this stretch, thick, leafy trees and plants of varied sort bordered the trail and hung over it, creating a green canopy above us as we walked. It was beautiful but eerie, seeing as there was no way of telling what might be lying in wait in the thick jungle. We drew our guns as we moved along, the trail growing increasingly narrow, funneling us into a single-file and making us even more vulnerable to an ambush. Sensing peril, Colonel Wood sent a couple of Cubans ahead to advance-scout. We waited long enough for them to return, only they didn't. We weren't sure why not. This added another ominous layer of uncertainty to the scene.

Soon, the trail turned into nothing more than a bridle path, with thick vegetation still rising up along its sides and bending above us to make a natural green roof, sparing us from the direct heat of the sun. Still, we sweat profusely from the heat and humidity.

Suddenly, Colonel Wood halted our movement and called our advance troop together. He told us—the fellas in Troop L—that we were to go ahead of the rest of the guys by a couple of hundred yards and reconnoiter. He seemed to instinctively sense something ahead.

We formed up, talked in hushed tones about our strategy, and advanced. As we worked our way along the trail, an odd-sounding "cuckoo" call came from the brush. We'd heard similar-sounding birds earlier in the day, especially in the morning, but this sounded a little peculiar and out of place.

"Could be them," Ton whispered back to me. I was about twenty feet behind him.

I kept my eyes peeled and kept walking. We heard another "cuckoo" call. Guys whispered up and down the line to each other, but no one seemed sure whether it was coming from a bird or a foe, let alone from exactly where within the thicket. Shortly thereafter, we heard it again. Then another time. Suddenly I saw the Cuban guide who'd been aiding Capron and Ton peel off and hightail it into the jungle, spooked.

We pushed on.

As we approached an area with high grass on the right flank and underbrush and a barbed wire fence on the left, the trail widened. Right at this point, Captain Capron and a part-Cherokee soldier named Tom Isbell, both of whom were at the front of our line, came upon a dead Spaniard lying in the middle of our trail. We crouched, senses on high alert, while Isbell bent down to investigate the dust-covered body. As he did, he glimpsed a Spanish soldier through the high grass and brush. With his carbine already primed, he quickly righted himself and pinked the Spaniard. A hail of Mauser bullets from other Spanish soldiers, who had been lying in wait in the gently rising high grass up ahead and to our left, came pouring down. Isbell got hit several times. His body shook, and then he went down. Seven bullets had riddled his body. Yet somehow he would survive.

At the sound of the gunfire, Culver, who wasn't far behind Isbell, had sprawled onto the ground and started firing away. For cover, he wedged up against the four inches of raised earth where our trail met the brush. Meanwhile, Ton, who was some thirty feet behind Culver when the shooting started, had rushed forward without hesitation. He looked like a wildcat unleashing every ounce of energy as he surged forward. When he reached Culver, he dove right up alongside him. They were lying at a diagonal in relation to our path, and by coming in on

Culver's side the way he did, what with the bulk of the Mauser fire coming from our left, Ton was now especially vulnerable.

"Old boy, you've got a good place here," Ton said ironically to Culver as the smokeless Spanish rifles continued to fire down bullets from all around. They both aimed their rifles and fired.

"That's right, old boy, a good place," Culver said, playing along.

I hate to admit it, but in these opening seconds of our first live action, I froze momentarily. My mind felt as if it had somehow left my body, as if it was observing things but no longer in control of its limbs. Shortly after this initial daze, though, I heard a voice rise up from the deep recesses of my mind. "Go, Rory, Go!"

At that I caught my bearings, dashed ahead, and dove headfirst alongside Ton and Culver. Ton eyed me and then grabbed the back of my uniform and yanked me over his body and Culver's so that his body would shield Culver's and mine from the bulk of the Spanish fire. There was no time to argue. Under the blazing sun, all three of us fired away.

Moments later, a high-pitched, whizzing sound turned into a sudden, abrupt *ummph*. Just as I turned to look at Ton, I felt something hit my upper chest, near the collarbone.

"Old boys, I'm wounded," Ton said, turning to us. "I'm badly wounded."

A bullet had entered Fish's right side, near where the rib cage and abdomen meet, and traveled out his left side before ricocheting off the top of Culver's shoulder and ripping through my skin just below my collarbone, lodging in my shoulder. Blood started to stain my uniform. I wasn't mortally wounded, but I did have a nasty gash. I was more worried about Ton.

"Ton?" I asked, scared and barely aware of a bullet whizzing by.

Fortunately, more Rough Riders had rushed forward and fanned out to engage the enemy, taking pressure off us.

Ton nodded grimly and turned to Culver, who was trying to put pressure on Ton's side to stop the bleeding. "Give me your canteen, old boy," Ton said. Culver did so and was rewarded with a knowing smile.

"You're all right, old boy."

Ton looked at me next and said wryly, "You're not too bad yourself. I was proud to be your second. You give 'em hell, Rory Mac, you hear me?"

I nodded, tears streaming down my cheeks.

Then Ton's eyes got heavy, his head fell slowly into his arms, and moments later he was gone. I grabbed the back of Ton's head with one arm and put my head near his as tears rolled down my cheeks.

He was the first Rough Rider killed in the Spanish-American War. One of America's brightest, one of its bravest, one of its most celebrated bachelors, killed on the outskirts of a small Cuban town, fighting for Cubans he did not know, serving as a shield for a poor kid from Hell's Kitchen and an even poorer young man from Muskogee Territory.

I was bleeding pretty badly. Culver was too—he'd been hit by a second bullet in the upper arm. I just lay there, holding onto Ton, faintly aware that Rough Riders were now surging ahead in waves. Several minutes must have passed, and I was losing blood. I began to drift in and out of consciousness.

Trying hard to stay conscious, I looked at the St. Joseph pendant that Ton had given me. I thought about the first time I'd met Ton, when he asked me to be his second. I thought about how he'd encouraged me to take my mom to dinner because he knew she didn't have anyone else who would. I thought about how hard he'd worked to train me to fight, how badly he'd wanted me to battle, to succeed. And I wondered why someone who could've been on a yacht off the coast of Newport at that very moment, enjoying a luxurious lifestyle the likes of which kids in Hell's Kitchen and Havana could only dream of, had decided to come to the frontline to help Cuba win freedom, to help someone like Carmen.

It was the thought of Carmen, in fact, that motivated me to try to stand up, to keep taking the fight to the enemy. But I only got to my knees before I passed out.

Chapter 26

As I say, it didn't take a veteran soldier to realize that the conditions along this part of the trail had been ripe for an ambush. But then again, seeing as we were the advance guard and our job was to locate the Spanish troops, I suppose "ambush" isn't the right word. I mean, part of our job was to snuff out the enemy, maybe even get them to show themselves. I bring this up because after the war critics liked to say that we were ambushed. Yet we knew the Spanish were lurking out there—Cuban rebels who had engaged them the day before had told us as much—and we knew that in trying to pinpoint the Spaniards' location, we might very well draw them out.

After the war, a fellow from Troop K, Ed Coakley, said it best. "Rory Mac," he said, "these loons calling it an ambush don't know a thing. That first night was no ambush, no how, whether it was a surprise party or not; and any fool who says that we were decoyed into an ambush, and that the Rough Riders didn't know they were to do any fighting that day, why, he is a liar—and there isn't a man in the regiment who wouldn't say it to his face, no matter how great a man he thinks himself."

Shortly after the initial firefight which took Ton's life, Colonel Wood ordered a group, led by Roosevelt, to charge through the thick brush and go right at the heart of the Mausers. Teddy tore through the Cuban terrain with abandon even as Spanish soldiers engaged him and his fellow Rough Riders. One bullet, I'd learn later, flew just above Roosevelt's head before hitting a nearby tree. He pushed on, and in time we gained the upper hand, causing the Spanish to pull back and reconfigure their position.

I'm told an hour passed before Culver and I were carried away by a medic, to a shaded area removed from the action. It was there that Dr. Church dressed our wounds.

I remember asking Dr. Church, "How bad is it?"

"You're going to make it, Rory Mac."

"Please don't send me back to camp," I said. "Let me heal here."

"You can't fight anymore, Rory," Doc said. "Your wound is too deep. If it's to heal without infection, you will have to take considerable care."

"I've got to get Ton, Doc. I've got to bury him," I said before drifting away again.

I recall little about the rest of that day. When I would drift into consciousness, I reminded myself of two simple things over and over: *Bury Ton. Find Carmen.* And I took comfort in hearing, late that night, that the rest of the Rough Riders, helped by the brave African-Americans of the Tenth Calvary, had forced the Spaniards into a full-on retreat.

***

The next morning I felt better, good enough to stand and eat eggs and hardtack. Doc told me Ton's body had been moved some 200 yards from where he had been killed, along a grassy hillside. If I felt up to it and didn't overdo it, I could watch the fellows dig his grave.

Culver, who'd lost less blood and healed quicker, walked with me a few hundred yards to Ton's body, near which Teddy, Woodbury, Buckey, and a couple of others had already started digging. They nodded at us solemnly. Ton's body was wrapped on the ground some twenty feet away, alongside the six others killed in action.

I felt like I should contribute something. So, with a

heavy heart and a foggy head, I grabbed a shovel and, using my strong arm, pushed the shovel blade into the side of the hill. For the next several minutes we dug in silence. While we dug, buzzards circled overhead, as if they needed to remind us how ruthless life can be.

When the hole was large enough for seven men, the uninjured fellows started setting the fallen bodies in. Along with Ton, there was an Indian, a cowboy, a miner, a packer, a former college athlete from the plains, and a Westerner whose background I did not know. Ton was the last to go in, and I was determined to be one of the men who carried him into the unmarked grave. Before we did so, I went over to him and pulled back the blanket that had been wrapped tightly around him. I knelt and looked at his strong jaw and eyes. Tears started to stream down my cheeks. I raised my left hand and made a boxing fist—you know, put my dukes up—and then gently moved my hand toward Ton's cheek, giving him an ever-so-soft tap. Then I pulled the blanket back over his head.

Several of us picked up Ton by the shoulders while others raised him by the legs. As we placed him gently into the unmarked grave with his fellow fallen comrades, I thought of the Hawthorne quote saying our bodies are just jugs carrying spirits.

We placed heavy fan palms, like the ones the Cubans had given us for our dog-tents when we first landed, on the bodies and shoveled soil back into the hole. Then we planted several saplings. We set additional fan palms down around the saplings before shoveling in a final layer of soil. We took considerable care.

When we'd finished, Buckey turned to Roosevelt and asked, "Colonel, isn't it Whitman who says of the vultures that 'they pluck the eyes of princes, and tear the flesh of kings'?"

We stood mostly in silence for a few minutes. For some reason, I started thinking about the time Ton had Culver dress up like him at that train stop in Lafayette. I couldn't help but smile through the tears, remembering how much of a kick Ton got out of that.

Right about this time, I'd learn later, Ton's mother was smiling through tears, too. Her heart ached, of course, in a way that only the heart of a mother who has lost a child can. Since news of Ton's death had arrived, she'd had a stream of condolatory telegrams, notes, and visitors to their home in Manhattan. Reporters were among the visitors; the papers had devoted reams of ink to her son's passing. But now she'd found time to go to her bedroom to grieve alone, and she'd found a Christmas wish list that Ton had written when he was just a child. It read,

Dear Santa Claus:

Please send to me one ape, two dogs, one giraffe and a small goat—all alive.

Hamilton Fish

Back on the hill where we'd put Ton and his comrades to rest, a young reverend, Henry W. Brown, arrived for the interment. He wore common, mud-stained canvas overalls and an old gray soldier's shirt. It was clear he'd had some long days and nights. I'd learn that just a little more than a month before, Reverend Brown had resigned his post as the rector of an Episcopal Church to become an Army chaplain. And now this burial was one of forty-four over which he'd preside in a two-day period.

At the end of the modest service, he said, "'Let us

pray." We removed our hats and got down on our knees in the mud.

***

Culver and I were put on limited duty to heal from our bullet wounds. We'd protested, but Doc had insisted. He said the wounds could open again and get infected. He would not release us for at least several days.

The rest of the day we didn't do much of anything other than lie on our makeshift cots in the temporary aid station. Here and there, we helped medics and supply men with odds and ends.

General Shaftner hadn't yet ordered the Army to continue forward, so the uninjured troops weren't far ahead of us. During downtime, Doc Church and his staff filled me in on the parts of the battle I'd missed. We'd apparently gotten in a pretty tight spot but, as I mentioned, with the help of the Tenth Cavalry, managed victory. Eight Rough Riders had been killed on the first day of fighting, thirty-one wounded. The Tenth suffered almost as many injuries. And two of its soldiers had been taken as prisoners. The troops were now awaiting orders to take Santiago.

Marshall, one of our embedded journalists, stopped by the medic station in the evening. He told me that the Red Cross, led by Clara Barton, was setting up a base of operations in Santiago. The Red Cross had been trying to do this for months, but convincing the Spanish to let them deliver food and medical supplies to desperate citizens in and around Santiago, some of whom the Spanish considered the enemy, had proven extremely difficult. Apparently, the force of Clara Barton's will had finally made it happen.

That night, we got permission to visit the active

Rough Riders. Their camp wasn't much better off than the one we were staying in. Fever was ripping through the ranks, and the spoiled meat that fellows had eaten on the *Yucatan* had weakened their immune systems.

Before I fell asleep, back at the medic camp, the prospect of lazing around the next few days tore me up.

I turned to Culver and, talking low, said, "I can't just lie around waiting for Doc Church to release me, hoping I don't catch fever, not learning anything new about Carmen, doing basically nothing. I'm going to find some way to help folks. Maybe I can be of some use to the Red Cross and in the process get closer to finding Carmen."

"You serious?" Culver asked.

"I can't just stay here. Ton wouldn't."

"They'll charge you with desertion."

"I don't care."

I simply couldn't sit there any longer, penned in, thinking about Ton's death and worrying about Carmen.

"Finding your way on foreign soil, living off the land, won't be easy. Do you know what you're getting yourself into?"

"I'll survive."

Culver took a deep breath. He was thinking things through. He turned to me, looked me dead in the eye, and asked, "When are we leaving?"

"Tonight."

He nodded.

Several hours later, deep into the night, we slipped out of our makeshift cots. We took with us a few medical supplies to clean and re-dress our wounds, and we brought along our machetes, Krag-Jorgensens, and pistols.

Before leaving, I slid a letter into Doc Church's tent.

It read:

Look, Doc, seeing as I'm of no use here, I've made up my mind to leave camp. I need to find a way to help. Culver came along because he's inactive, too, and he thinks it's his duty to protect me. Please don't hold him accountable for me being the darnedest ass in this regiment.

Respectfully,
Rory Mac

Culver and I didn't have an exact plan worked out. We moved carefully through the dark, not wanting to come upon any Spanish soldiers. But we weren't too worried about them seeing as our medic station was about eight miles from downtown Santiago and most of the Spanish soldiers in this part of Cuba were stationed closer to the city center, on high ground, in hills such as San Juan and Kettle. At least, this is what we'd heard from other Rough Riders. We determined it was more likely for us to come across Cubans, and all of the Cubans we'd encountered up to then had been eager to help us. We hoped we'd run into someone who could tell us where to find the Red Cross.

The terrain we traversed presented some difficulties, though, since we didn't want to take any main trails and therefore made our way through dim, overgrown paths. If we ran into a dead end, we simply cut our way through the thick foliage until we picked up another dim trail, all the while keeping a lookout for any signs, smoke or otherwise, of one of the many small villages that dotted Santiago's outskirts.

A few miles into our mission, walking along a trail that cut through the jungle in a curvy fashion—with occasional forks that we guessed at—we caught a break. The sun was just starting to rise when we encountered a young man about my age, walking slowly ahead of us. With our guns drawn, we called after him.

He turned and raised his hands, and we motioned for him to come toward us. As he got close, it was clear to us that he was unarmed and not a threat. I dropped my gun and held out my hand. He shook it nervously and told us his name was Escobar.

When he realized that we did not intend to hurt him, he brought his hands to his mouth, intimating that he wanted food. We tried to tell him that we were looking for the Red Cross, but I don't think he understood. He waved us ahead, as if to say, "Follow me." On instinct, we obliged.

We walked along a tiny path that cut through a heavy stretch of some 200 meters of jungle-like terrain, after which it opened to a field, dotted with 50 or so one-room huts. These huts, glorified tents really, with palm-leaf thatched roofing, had been built throughout Cuba to house the *reconcentrados*. This camp had apparently been abandoned by the Spanish, but, having been uprooted from their homes and left with virtually nothing, some of the Cubans sent here had remained. They no longer had anywhere else to go, let alone the means to get there.

They'd sent out the healthiest among them, Escobar, to hunt or scavenge or journey downtown to get what he could. It was overwhelming to think that even if we got these people food, which would take us hours to accomplish, by day's end they'd be hungry all over again.

And not just them. People all over Cuba faced similar conditions.

As we passed an abandoned military blockhouse, Escobar motioned us over and pushed open the front door. I tentatively stepped forward and peered inside. There were twenty or so people, young and old, in tragically desperate shape. One mother, lying on the floor, had her arm weakly around two listless children. All three were emaciated, with distant eyes. There were flies all over their bodies. The other people in the blockhouse were in the same condition or worse. One or two appeared already dead. It was gut-wrenching to see.

This blockhouse had become a place of quarantine to protect the others. I started to step inside, but Escobar pulled me back. He knew enough about sickness and death to know the room was pestilent. He also knew that there were other hungry Cubans in the nearby huts who would soon be sent to this blockhouse if help didn't arrive soon.

Sure, food sent to Cuba by the U.S. government and the Red Cross, as well as other charitable organizations, had helped to improve the situations in *reconcentrados* in and around Havana, but issues with transportation, communication, and safety had kept resources from arriving in makeshift camps like this one. And, as I said, there were many such camps throughout Cuba.

Escobar knocked on one of the huts. A man came to the door and spoke to Escobar for a few moments. Culver and I glanced nervously at each other. Escobar brought this man over to us. "*Carlos, Ingles,*" he said, to let us know that this man spoke or at least understood English.

Culver and I did our best to explain to Carlos that we

needed to get to Santiago, to the city center, and that we wanted to let the Red Cross know about this camp. He nodded and went back inside. His wife appeared with native garments in hand and Carlos motioned for us to put them on. They thought it best if we dressed like locals to avoid attention.

With our weapons strapped to our bodies, we set off for the city center with Escobar and the last mule they could spare. As we neared the center of Santiago, I worried that a Spanish sympathizer would spot us, especially when a few children started following us, asking for food or money. We kept on, and nearer the city center Escobar got directions to the Red Cross station from a local. We were only a mile away.

A shipment of food had arrived that day, so when we arrived, hundreds of people were lined up outside what had recently been turned into the Red Cross building. We saw sacks of food being loaded onto mules and taken away under the protection of U.S. soldiers. We figured the Red Cross must've worked a security arrangement out with both sides of the war, allowing food to be delivered, and that the food was heading for hungry, smaller communities on the edges of the city, like Escobar's. We fought our way toward the waiting mules and pleaded for help.

"We have a mule," I told a soldier. "We'll protect the food, if you could just please give us some."

My wound had started to seep blood and a little fluid. I saw that the soldier noticed. I pulled aside the shirt Escobar had lent me to show him my blood-stained Rough Rider shirt and said, "There are some people out there who need our help." I explained the location from which we came and to which we needed to get food.

"Take those," he said, pointing to two heavy sacks of rice and grain. Then he grabbed two smaller sacks, one filled with canned meat, the other with hardtack, and gave them to us.

"Thank you," I said, placing the sacks on the back of our mule. "Do you know where I can find Clara Barton?"

"She's in there," he said, pointing to a small structure about a hundred feet away.

"Keep moving, I'll catch up with you," I told Culver and Escobar.

I knocked and stepped inside Clara Barton's office. The matronly seventy-seven-year-old, with her curly hair pulled back in a bun, met me with a smile.

"How can I help you?" she asked.

"Hello, ma'am. Sorry to interrupt, but I have a problem that I hope you can help me with."

"I'll do my best. What is it?"

I told her everything: that I was a Rough Rider, that I'd fallen in love with Carmen, that she had stayed in Cuba to take care of her father, that she'd been captured and put into either a prison or a *reconcentrado*, and that I desperately needed to find her.

"I thought, perhaps, with your connections, that you could make some inquiries on my behalf?" I said. "I would be eternally grateful."

"I'll see what I can do. Come back here tomorrow. Same time."

"Thank you," I said, bowing slightly.

I hustled back to Culver, Escobar, and our mule. They were going slowly on my behalf, so it didn't take long to catch up with them. We decided to find a secluded patch of forest and wait for nightfall. We figured this way bandits would be less likely to spot our supplies.

When darkness fell, Escobar led us through a series of paths in the forest. Occasionally we stepped out onto a stretch of unpaved road. We walked in silence for a few hours.

Even though it was late when we arrived, people came out of their huts when they realized we had food. We set up a little table and Culver, Escobar, and I divvied everything up into equal portions. It wasn't a huge amount per person, but they could stretch what we gave them over a few days, and they were grateful for it.

The toughest part came when we went over to the quarantined blockhouse. We wanted to give the folks inside some food, but we knew the risk of getting sick ourselves. We determined that we'd hustle in and set portions next to them, in the hopes that they could muster the energy to eat. Several of them couldn't. Seeing the children unable to even lift food to their mouths was heart-rending. By candlelight and despite the risk of sickness, we decided to spoon-feed these children. They could barely muster the energy to chew.

Then we carried a mother and child that had died the day prior to the forest and gave them a proper burial.

Chapter 27

The sun was nearly rising when we finally lay down on the ground to sleep. A few hours later, Culver and I awoke to Escobar roasting coffee. We packed up our gear, relished some hot coffee, and started walking downtown. We figured we'd help the Red Cross folks as best we could until my appointment with Clara Barton.

On our way into town, Escobar angled us through the jungle so that we passed another desperate village of one-room, palm-leafed huts and a quarantined block-house. Twenty yards from this blockhouse, I saw a mass grave that was many times bigger than the one we'd dug for Ton. A few men from different huts stepped outside, and Escobar went over to them. He spoke with them for several minutes before we continued on our way. I could tell from their hushed tones and the way they huddled up that they were talking about something important, but I didn't try to figure out what. I trusted Escobar now and figured his business was his business.

At the Red Cross station, we helped carry sacks of rice to the backs of already tired mules until it came time for my appointment with Miss Barton.

When I stepped into her office, she looked tired, like she'd put in a long night. I'm sure many things were on her mind. She remembered our meeting from the previous day. She stood up from her desk and we exchanged a greeting. Then she put her hand on my shoulder, and said, "Rory Mac, I made inquiries, and I've got some news for you."

"Yes ma'am," I said eagerly.

"Carmen is in Santiago," she said. My heart nearly beat out of my chest.

"Do you know where exactly?" I asked.

"What I've been told is that, awhile back, she was taken to a prison on the outskirts of Santiago, while her father was sent to one in Camaguey. Apparently, the Spanish thought they'd get less attention if they moved them away from Havana. My contact had no other information. I'm sorry."

I stepped forward and hugged her. "Oh, thank you. I'm near her," I said. "You don't know how grateful I am. Thank you."

I left and immediately found a Red Cross nurse who spoke English and a little Spanish and asked her to explain the situation to Escobar, and to see if he could use his contacts to get more information. Escobar said he would try.

Wherever she was being held would be heavily guarded, I assumed, which meant that the best shot at getting in was for the U.S. Army to gain control of Santiago. I needed to get back to the Rough Riders and help them take this city. My wound was doing better, and I figured it would only be another day or so until I could expect Doc Church to release me to active duty—that is, if I wasn't court-martialed for going AWOL.

Our translator's Spanish was quite rudimentary, but she managed to explain to Escobar that Culver and I planned to return to our regiment and that we hoped to help the rebels win back Santiago. In the meantime, I asked that, were he to receive information on Carmen, he find me and share it with me. Through the translator, he told us he understood and that he would accompany us back to his village. Then we could continue on to our Rough Rider camp. Culver and I nodded in agreement. As we loaded our mule for the return trip, Escobar took the Red Cross nurse by the arm and said something to her with an earnest look on his face.

"He wants to tell you something," our translator said.

"Okay," I said, looking at Escobar as he talked to the translator.

"He says that you have helped his people survive, that he will forever be grateful for this and that he will do everything he can to find out where Carmen is being held. He wants you to know that when he does find out, he will locate you and tell you immediately."

"*Gracias*," I said to Escobar, reaching out to shake his hand.

"*De nada.*"

***

That night, having waited again for darkness, Escobar, Culver, and I made the seven-or eight-mile walk through thick jungle back to his community. After helping Escobar unpack the mule and distribute the food, we parted ways, and a short time later Culver and I arrived at camp.

The sun was an hour or so from rising, and yet we found Doc Church, who always rose early, under a canvas canopy, double-checking medical supplies and making sure everything was in order before the day got underway. I worried that he'd be quite angry at us. He looked at us disapprovingly, but seeing how tired and ragged we must've looked, ushered us to recovery cots.

The moment Culver and I hit our cots, we passed out from exhaustion. Sometime later, Doc Church came by for rounds. I wasn't sure exactly what to say, about us having left and all, but he made it easy on us by acting like nothing had happened. He simply cleaned our wounds, asked how we were feeling, and then marked our paperwork. Before moving on to wake-up his next patient, he leaned in toward Culver and me and said quietly, "You're free to return to the front, fellas. Take care, now." Then he gave us a look that said, "I respect what you did, and I covered for you. Now go take care of business, and don't ever pull a stunt like that again." I figured he'd had a talk with Teddy, and they'd decided to let it go.

At the front, Culver and I found that the Rough Riders, frustrated as all get-out, were still waiting for General Shafter to order them to Santiago.

"You two dandies finally feelin' better?" Buckey O'Neil joked.

"Reckon we're aright," Culver said.

"Wouldn't much matter if you warn't anyhow," Buckey replied. "They got us penned in with nothin' to do but bake in this here sun."

Within hours, however, the directive to take Santiago arrived.

Chapter 28

General Wheeler had succumbed to fever; this meant Dr. Wood came into command of the Second Brigade, and Teddy officially became our colonel. He'd wanted to move on Santiago right away, so was pleased to receive General Shafter's orders. He wasn't pleased, however, with the order's lack of specifics. He worried that General Shafter did not have the Rough Riders playing an important role in the siege of the city.

By midafternoon, we'd packed everything up and moved into formation. When the call to march bellowed down the line, our hearts quickened. But, in classic Army fashion, after we'd only gone a few hundred yards we received orders to stop and wait until someone told us to start again. While we sat and waited in the scorching heat on a narrow pathway, several regular Army regiments and raggedly-clothed Cuban insurgents passed by on their way to Santiago, making it quite clear that the Army didn't have us playing a lead role in the assault. Teddy wasn't happy, nor was General Wood—who, even though he'd made Brigadier General and didn't have to, had joined us on the march.

When we finally got going again, we made steady progress. Now and again, a plug in the line ahead would force us to stop and wallow in the heat. Occasionally, we'd wade across a stream, giving us the opportunity to cool down. When nighttime came, and with thick jungle on either side of our path, it got a little spooky, worrying about an ambush. But eventually we made it to El Poso Hill. Considering we had horses pulling our Gatling guns and a mass of supplies, we'd made good time.

Army scouts had reported back that the area around

El Poso was safe, so we marched to the top and set up camp near an abandoned sugar factory and dilapidated ranch. We were so tired we simply lined up by troop, dropped our belongings, and lay on the ground for sleep.

Culver started in on one of his stories about growing up on the range, and next thing I knew, a soft bugle marked reveille, awaking us before the sun got its chance. Culver, ever resourceful, had gotten his hands on some beans and coffee, even some sugar. This was a nice complement to our three-day supply of hardtack and bacon. He and I and a couple others from our troop made a modest fire to heat the bacon and roast the coffee.

As the sun rose, its rays brightened the lush green valley below and revealed up ahead, on a hill closer to Santiago, the battery of U.S. field guns that had been set up. Army regulars on this hill were moving into position. Beyond them, I could glimpse the land upon which the main part of Santiago sat, ringed as it was by thick green mountains.

Our latest orders, if you want to call them that, had arrived. Really, they amounted to a general explanation of what we were to do next: create a diversion with our artillery while General Lawton and his men engaged the Spanish at El Caney, a town a couple of miles or so to our right, just outside of Santiago. In other words, they'd do the real fighting, and we'd fire shells to back them up.

Tiffany, Woodbury, and the rest of Troop K positioned the artillery guns, and a short time later the booming sound of cannons vibrated from El Caney to us, letting us know the game was afoot. Troop K fired artillery shots at the Spanish positions to our right.

It worked to our advantage to have the high ground, but it also meant that we were quite visible. Soon, smokeless blasts from Spanish artillery guns, the location of which was hard to pinpoint, began landing near us. Indeed, two shells, accompanied by only a high-pitched whistling sound, exploded some twenty feet from Culver and me, rattling the earth all around us. Seconds later, more shells exploded in the air directly above us, and still more a little ways off.

At the sound of the enemy fire, Teddy Roosevelt jumped on his horse and ordered us to take cover in thick underbrush just below the crest of El Poso hill. As I went for cover, I looked to my right and saw that a group of Cuban insurgents who'd joined us on the hilltop had suffered a direct hit.

Several fellows in our troop were letting out shrieks of pain. They'd been hit by shrapnel from the exploding artillery shells. A particularly gnarly clutch of shrapnel had torn into Smokin' Joe's leg, nearly ripping the limb from his body. And shards had ripped through the horse upon which General Wood was mounted.

As we took cover and the Spanish fire lulled, we knew we needed a better plan of action. Otherwise, we'd spend the rest of the day sitting near El Poso's crest, susceptible to enemy fire, while not providing much cover for General Lawton's men. Especially since our guns were slow to fire.

We columned-up and listened to Teddy bark orders. We were to move around to the side of the hill and start angling downward to our right, toward a shallow portion of the San Juan River. We knew we'd be fired at along the way, but at least we'd be moving and configuring ourselves to take the action to the Spaniards.

Our vague orders had suggested that at some point we should connect with Lawton's troops. No timeline or clear meeting point had been given, let alone guidance on the whereabouts and size of the enemy in the vicinity. So Teddy's nature took over. If he didn't have enough information, he would look for it. If his orders lacked clarity, he'd provide it. When in doubt, he preferred to take the action to the enemy rather than wait for the enemy to bring the action to him. Thus, we moved downward to the ford, toward the enemy, into fire.

Upon reaching the ford, we crossed the San Juan under fire. It was intense. We marched rightward another half-mile toward cover to await further direction. Our journey to this point had highlighted the ruthlessness and randomness that accompanies battle. A man ten feet in front of you or five feet behind you might go down in a flash, felled by a nearly soundless bullet. Shrapnel from a smokeless artillery shell might startle you by pricking your forearm, as it did mine, while another piece of shrapnel from the same shell might very well sever an artery in the neck of a soldier three people removed from you. There's scant time in the thick of the battle to dwell on such things. Continuing to move, keeping an eye out for cover, occasionally returning fire, take precedence.

Having found cover for the time being, we saw one of our scout balloons, sent to the skies to observe Spanish movements, come back down to the ground. It'd started wavering a few minutes earlier and had descended in a wavy path back to its tethered stakes, which were, unfortunately, right near our position. Since the balloon could serve as a kind of guide for the Spanish to our position, we pressed on.

It was inspiring to see Woodbury and Tiffany's troop somehow still pulling our massive Gatling gun. Still under fire, we came to a sunken lane, near the foot of Kettle

Hill. Culver and I and several others took cover in the thick jungle grass at the bottom of the hill, while others took cover by digging into the bank of the nearby San Juan River. By this time regular Army troops had melded with us, so it was a bit of a mishmash as far as regiments go.

Teddy sent two men to scuttle back to receive our next orders. He told them to tell his superiors that he wanted the order to charge. Initially, nothing came of this effort. In the meantime, our position became increasingly perilous. Men were getting hit by fire, some killed. We weren't in a position to fire effectively, so we just got down low—or most of us did. Every now and then I'd catch a glimpse of Buckey O'Neil walking back and forth, smoking a cigarette, carrying on under the misguided notion that officers shouldn't take cover. Now and again, he'd inform us of the direction of the Spanish fire or just generally try to motivate us. "Buckey, you need to get down, you crazy ole mule," Culver called out.

"The Spanish bullet isn't made that will kill me," Buckey said at one point. But he was wrong. Several minutes later, he took a bullet through the mouth. It killed him instantly.

Finally, one of Teddy's messengers came back saying that we'd been given the go-ahead to charge Kettle Hill. *This is it,* I thought; *the time to act is upon us.*

A colonel in charge of some of the regular Army troops that had mixed in with us sent in an order for us to start slowly crawling up the hill. He wanted us to stay low and fire when we could. Teddy didn't like this strategy one bit. He powered his horse to the back of our line to recommend to a lieutenant colonel that we commence a full-on charge. When Teddy saw that the colonel who'd ordered the crawl was not on the battlefield, he declared himself the ranking officer and then ordered the charge. As he did, he turned his horse toward the hill and started galloping up it. My word, did he make for an impressive sight.

Inspired, Culver and I and the rest of the Rough Riders, as well as the regular soldiers in our vicinity, stood upright and charged. Just as we did, as if on cue, General Parker's Gatlin guns suddenly fired behind us. They'd been raised on a slight slope near the bottom of the hill and were pointed directly at the Spanish trenches at the top.

"The Gatlins, the Gatlins!" we all shouted excitedly as we stormed Kettle Hill.

A group of soldiers to the left of us had lain in wait as we rushed. When we took cover a hundred yards or so up the hill, they rose and rushed ahead. When they took cover, it was our turn to surge again. All the while, Teddy rode his horse up and down our line, urging us on, unconcerned about the Mauser bullets whizzing by. Within twenty minutes, the hill was ours—thanks largely to sheer will, and the Gatlins, of course, we'd pushed the Spanish back.

There were sugar-refining kettles atop Kettle Hill. We used them as shields while we provided cover fire for the soldiers now storming San Juan Hill, which was right next to us. These soldiers made it to the top, as well, and by day's end we'd captured the ring of hills known as the San Juan Heights, giving us a considerable advantage.

Within forty-eight hours, the Spanish cruiser fleet stationed in and around Santiago fell to the U.S. Navy, putting Spain in an even more precarious position. Practically speaking, it'd lost Santiago, even if it didn't surrender. Over the next couple of weeks, Spain mounted only the occasional skirmish, which it usually lost.

***

When I'd heard that the Spanish cruiser fleet had fallen and realized that all the Rough Rider regiment was likely to do for some time was wait in camp, I decided it was time to find Carmen. I set out that afternoon on foot and came upon Escobar on a nearby trail. He'd left his people the night before to find me, just as he'd said he would. As he walked up, we embraced.

"Carmen is in El Morro," he said, haltingly.

"El Morro?" I asked, not sure where that was.

Escobar nodded and then started moving his arms, trying to explain something to me that he did not know how to say in English.

"*Un momento*," I said. "*Un momento*."

I dashed back to camp to get Burt Mossman, a fellow Rough Rider who knew a little Spanish. With Burt in tow, I hustled back to Escobar.

"Carmen is being held in El Morro," Mossman explained to me as he translated for Escobar. "It's like a fortress, a former castle. It sits where the Caribbean Sea meets the Santiago Bay, about ten kilometers from here. Rebels are planning to attack it tonight. They have a man on the inside and now that Santiago has nearly fallen, they're going in. It's no longer heavily guarded. Carmen is thought to be there. Do you want to come?"

"Of course, I do," I said, picking Escobar up for a bear hug. "Yes, of course. *Si, señor*."

I knew I'd have to square this with Teddy, so I went to his makeshift office. I found him under a canvas roof, sitting in a chair, looking over a map setting on a small desk. I'd mentioned Carmen to him, of course, on our train ride into New Orleans; so he knew the gist. Now I told him that she was a mere seven miles away, in El Morro.

"You love her, do you?" he asked me.

"Very much so, sir."

"Santiago will eventually fall, you know, we can be most assured of this now."

"Yes, I know. But we can't be sure how long it will take for the Spanish to actually surrender. There could be many more weeks of fighting, perhaps months. I fear for her health as well as her safety," I said.

Teddy picked his head up a bit and looked out toward the horizon. Perhaps at that moment he thought about his first wife, who had died of typhoid fever at a young age, and how badly he'd have liked to see her again.

"You trust this Escobar?" Teddy asked.

I nodded. He thought deeply for several more moments before finally saying, "You can go. Be back for reveille in the morning. We will not speak of it again."

"Yes, sir. And thank you."

***

Escobar and I waited for nightfall before setting off. We stayed on trails the first several miles, avoiding the main roads. Even though the Spanish were reeling and pretty much holed up in Santiago, we still had to be careful.

Within a mile or two of El Morro, we pulled out our machetes, got off the beaten path, and took to the jungle. It wasn't easy slicing our way through the thick undergrowth and the foliage hanging off the various jungle bushes and trees.

Eventually, we cut our way through and stepped out

to a vast stretch of rocky shoreline which led to the Caribbean Sea. To our right, about 200 yards away, was the Bay of Santiago. On a wedge of land where these two bodies of water met, sat the imposing El Morro prison.

Escobar and I worked our way over to a large boulder. There we found a handful of rebels, crouching quietly. Alongside them was a rectangular crate about three feet long, with what looked like dynamite inside. Escobar found the man who appeared to be the leader of this group. The man looked displeased at first to see me, but his demeanor softened as Escobar explained why I was there. When Escobar finished, the man nodded my way in solidarity.

Crouching low, we scampered to a handful of smaller boulders about a hundred feet ahead. From there, the three rebels in charge of the explosives quickly slid the dynamite crate to a small cluster of bushes just outside El Morro's southern wall, which was several stories high and about a hundred yards long. Behind this portion of the wall were holding cells. Having positioned the dynamite, these soldiers hustled back to us, with the fuse line trailing behind.

One of the rebels then aimed his rifle at the lone guard who was pacing back and forth atop El Morro's southern wall. This Spanish guard, feeling the warning shot whizz past his ear, dropped his rifle. He knew, I'm sure, how lightly guarded the prison now was. No reason to lose his life over a war that had already basically been lost.

Then came the blast. It was terribly powerful. We waited several moments before hustling to the hole in the side of the prison created by the explosion. We had extra rifles with us to hand to escaping prisoners. Within moments we heard rebels emerging from the rubble. Rifle fire came from inside while more rebels poured out.

Escobar and I, now in the holding area, shouted at the escaping prisoners, *"Donde es Carmen? Donde es Carmen Castilla?"*

One of the escapees stopped for a moment, grabbed Escobar by the shoulder, said something quickly, and continued his mad dash to freedom. Escobar looked at me. I could see he was worried, but he waved me ahead further into the prison.

It was practically empty now. Two guards had been shot, not fatally, but they'd been slowed enough to be disarmed and, like the man on the roof, they'd now resigned themselves to the prison break. Moving down a hallway, we came to the door of what seemed to be a large holding cell, but discovered that the door was barred shut from the inside.

Escobar found a smaller cell nearby. He grabbed a key dangling nearby from the wall and tried it on this cell door. It unlocked. The smell inside was awful. I immediately saw a dead man lying on a cot. He had the tell-tale signs of having succumbed to yellow fever. This, then, was the quarantine room. Straight ahead lay a woman in bad shape, probably on account of typhoid fever.

Then I looked to my right and saw Carmen, emaciated, lifeless. I stepped quickly toward her and put my hand to her cheek. There was no doubt. She was dead. I dropped to my knees and sobbed.

I don't know how long I kneeled there holding Carmen in my arms. I vaguely heard Escobar say something to me, but it didn't register. Nothing seemed to matter. I felt utter, complete devastation. The impact of Ton's death and now Carmen's had knocked me flat.

Several minutes must've passed before I heard a voice from the deep recesses of my brain say, "Get up, Rory Mac. Get up!" Memories of Ton and Carmen came to me, memories of when they were strong and spirited. And I heard the voice again, "Get up, Rory Mac."

Only then did I realize that Escobar was pulling on my shoulder, saying "*Vamanos, vamanos.*"

I picked up Carmen's body and put her across my shoulders. I carried her out of the prison, over the rocks and sand and out into the jungle.

I don't remember much about the next several hours, but I do know that a mile or so into the jungle Escobar visited a small, dilapidated village of huts. Having awakened a man he knew, he borrowed a shovel, and then, mostly through motioning to me, explained that we needed to bury Carmen's body on the outskirts of this village. I understood his meaning. I didn't want to let her go, but I knew he was right. Her family could come back for her later.

When we finished digging the grave, we wrapped a few layers of thick palm leaves around her. I hugged her body tightly, and then we laid Carmen to rest.

Chapter 29

We traveled through the night and covered the miles it took to get back to the Rough Riders' camp just before sunup. Working on sheer adrenaline, my mind was numb, processing virtually nothing. I kept moving as if somehow movement alone could help me cope with the reality of Carmen's death. I was grateful that Escobar guided me the whole way.

Over the next couple of weeks, there was nothing to do other than wait at camp for the Spanish to surrender. It was nice to have Culver around, and Woodbury and Tiffany, but my mind remained shaken and dispirited. I was struggling like I never had before, grasping for a reason to keep on living. I thought about my mother, how I needed to be able to take care of her. This helped keep me going.

About a week in, telegrams and regular mail started to reach soldiers. This made me hopeful that the letters I'd sent to Evangelina and Ton's parents had reached their destinations. To Evangelina, I'd explained how we'd tried to save Carmen but had been too late. I told her that I loved her sister, and that my heart was broken. I described the burial we'd given Carmen and her location.

Seeing as Ton's death had elicited front-page coverage across America, his mother and father were aware of the main details. Still, I wanted the Fishes to hear from me how I felt about their son, how grateful I was that he'd lifted me up when I was a boy and helped to forge me into the man I was becoming. And I told them that he'd not only gone straight to the front and fought bravely; he'd saved my life and Culver's, too. I felt guilty writing to them, knowing that I was alive because of their son's sacrifice and yet he was gone. I worried that they wished he'd never met me.

A day or two before the Spanish formally surrendered Santiago, I received a telegram from Ton's father. He was coming to Cuba to bring Ton's body home. He wanted to know if I wanted to meet him in Siboney to help. Of course I did.

Before Mr. Fish's arrival, I received a letter from Carmen's father, who was now free. With a group of friends, he'd gone for his daughter, and had her exhumed and buried in Havana, in the same cemetery as her mother. It gave me comfort knowing this.

A couple days later, in the morning, I met in Siboney with Mr. Fish and the undertaker he'd traveled with, J.C. Burton. We rendezvoused with ten armed guards who were going to help us bring Ton back. We then began the several-mile-long trip to Las Guasimas, upon knotty roads that looked all too familiar. The hills in particular were tough to traverse. At one point, while climbing a particularly steep section of hill, Mr. Fish lost his footing and slid several feet downward, banging his left leg against jagged rock. He scraped his skin badly and endured a painful bone bruise. But he carried on.

Hours later, we arrived at the hillside upon which we'd buried Ton. It was here that Mr. Fish went ahead of us a bit and walked through the high grass before stopping to survey the land and gaze out to the horizon. We gave him some space before we started digging.

It took a few hours to unearth Ton. We'd taken care when we'd buried him, and now we took care in bringing him out of the mass grave. When we finished digging, Mr. Fish stepped forward, tears in his eyes, kneeled down to his son's body, and said, "You fought for what you thought was right, son."

Solemnly, we loaded Ton's body onto our military cart, wrapped as it was in a blanket and layers of thick palm leaves. Before leaving, we carefully re-filled the burial ground.

Mr. Fish was quiet all the way back to Siboney. Not until we were sailing away on the *Solace* did he begin to open up.

"He looked very much like his great-grandfather, Colonel Nicholas Fish, you know?" he said to me.

"Is that so?"

"It is. His great-grandfather entered the Army during the Revolutionary War at seventeen years old. I bet that's about your age, that right?"

"Yes, sir."

"You're brave for coming, Rory Mac," Mr. Fish said. "Ton told me you were brave." He was silent for several moments. "Thank you for coming with me today."

"Of course," I said.

He looked out to the sea. "Yes, he looked just like his great-grandfather."

***

The return of Ton's body to America was covered by newspapers from coast to coast, as was his subsequent funeral in New York.

The night before the funeral, I visited the Fishes. The flag outside their home flew at half-mast. They answered the door looking rather worn. Throughout the day they'd received numerous callers offering condolences. Tomorrow's funeral weighed heavily.

While I was there, a representative of the U.S. Army stopped in to ask Mr. Fish if he was okay with having six

Squadron A soldiers serve as pallbearers. The Fishes expressed their gratitude and accepted. They wanted a simple ceremony without an overly prominent military character. Still, they considered this an appropriate touch.

When morning broke, we moved Ton's coffin, adorned with an American flag, from Burton's undertaking establishment to St. Mark's Protestant Episcopal Church. St. Mark's was in the Bowery section of Manhattan, on Tenth Street and Second Avenue, the site of the original Stuyvesant family chapel, built in 1660. Ton's great-grandfather, in fact, had donated the land upon which St. Mark's sat, with the understanding that a chapel would again be built there. As we approached the church, we saw a mass of people outside. Folks were already arriving in anticipation of Ton's funeral. By the time it formally started, thousands had amassed outside. Onlookers couldn't get into the packed chapel, so they peered through the iron fence ringing St. Mark's lawn, hoping to see what they could. When this area became too crowded, folks gathered across the street. Clearly, Ton had touched something in people's hearts, something they could relate to, something authentic and purposeful.

In addition to the Fish family, scores of Delta Psi fraternity men and a dozen Rough Riders made it into the church for the service, including Culver, who'd arrived in the city that morning after a long journey from Cuba. On account of the Rough Riders' rugged clothing and haggard appearances, the people out on the streets knew who they were as they made their way into the church. And folks slapped them on the backs, shook their hands, and generally let them know how much they appreciated their service.

Those who couldn't attend the funeral could read

up on it in newspapers far and wide. They covered everything from the resplendent floral arrangements to the "Siegfried" funeral march, which was played as the Fish family walked to their seats accompanied by General Lloyd Bryce and the former New York City mayor, Edward Cooper.

After the service, we took Ton's coffin from St. Mark's to Grand Central Station, where we boarded a train for Garrison, New York. There we put Ton to rest on Fish family land known as the "Garrisons on the Hudson."

As Ton was laid in his final resting place, flanked by soldiers from Squadron A, an old man from the crowd stepped forward. He was dressed in the faded blue coat of the Union Army. He didn't need to say anything, nor did the soldiers of Squadron A. They simply acted like the old man was a member of their squad. Squadron A shot volleys into the air in commemoration of Ton's life. After that, "Taps" was played.

Chapter 30

I was forlorn for some time. In the coming days and weeks, I didn't know what to do other than go home, give my mom the money I'd saved, and lay in bed or walk Manhattan aimlessly. I thought about returning to the paper, giving them all that I'd written about the war, and going back to the beat, but I couldn't bring myself to do it. Instead, I simply sent a telegram saying I needed time.

One afternoon, a fellow knocked at the front door of our tenement. I pulled myself out of bed to find one of Mr. Fish's coachmen standing there. I knew I looked bad. After exchanging greetings, he handed me a pair of boxing gloves, which I recognized right away, and a letter. It was from Mr. Fish. When the coachman left, I peeled open the envelope:

Rory Mac,

I know times are hard, but I hope this letter finds you well. I hope that you will return to work soon and find happiness again. Thank you again for helping me bring Ton's body home.

We have settled his estate, and he left you two things. First, the boxing gloves. I know how much the sport meant to both of you, and I hope you know that your boxing helped pull my son up at a time when he was down. My wife and I will never forget that. Second, here is the title to Ton's investment in a silver mine in Arizona. He made it clear in his will that he wanted you to own this, free and clear. I took the liberty of arranging it so that any dividends from this investment go directly into a bank account set up in your name through a dear friend

of ours at the Riggs Bank. Hope you don't mind.
   Never lose your fighting spirit,
   Sincerely,
   Nicholas Fish

For weeks I'd felt down, but holding Ton's boxing gloves in my hand and the letter from his father brought forth a faint glimmer of hope. I still spent the next couple of weeks at home but, finally, in early September, I started to come out of my emotional stupor.

Soon after, content in knowing that the dividend from the silver mine Ton had left me would allow me to take care of my mom, I decided that I needed to head West, to start fresh in a new place. Based on what I'd heard from some of the Rough Riders I'd served with, I settled on California, where there was apparently good soil, natural beauty, and sunshine. First, though, I took the Nickel Plate to Chicago and then the Cannonball to Salt Lake City. Something inside me said I needed to go there, to see what Ton's life had been like out West, to follow his path, and to find Jane Witherspoon. I needed to tell her in person how Ton had lived since she'd last seen him, how he'd died, and how he'd loved her.

***

Arriving in Salt Lake, I took a room at the Knutsford Hotel, on the corner of State and South, put my things up, and went for a walk. My heart was heavy, but the Western air felt crisp and light. I walked several miles.

That night I grabbed a beer at a bar near the Knutsford, where I met an older fellow who was in a talkative disposition. I asked about the area, let him know I was new to town, and wound around to asking about Jane and the Witherspoons. He knew all about them, as did most folks in the Wasatch Valley. Her old man had died, he told me. Jane had been away for a while and the ranch had fallen into a state of disrepair. But she'd returned some months back and taken the ranch over. She was a different kind of woman, this fellow told me. I decided I'd stop by the ranch the next morning.

The sun had been up a few hours when I passed under the entranceway to the Witherspoon Ranch and climbed the gently sloping hill leading to the main house. It'd been a fine, long walk. This was beautiful country, deep blue streams, white-capped mountains, purple sage, brown rock.

I knocked on the door.

"Hello, how can I help you?"

Ton was right. Jane was a striking beauty.

"My name's Rory Mac, miss. I served with Ton Fish in the Rough Riders. I'm on my way west, to California. I thought I'd stop by."

"Yes, of course. Ton told me about you. Please come in. I'm glad you came."

"Thank you."

We walked to the kitchen.

"You been in town long?"

"No, miss. Came in on the Cannonball yesterday."

"Would you like some coffee? Are you hungry?"

"I suppose some coffee will do."

"And I'll fry up a little bacon. I planned to cook some anyway."

She went to the stove to heat water for the coffee and to place strips of bacon on the fryer.

"Ton told me a lot about you," I said. It was silent for a few moments.

She turned away from the fryer and toward me. Her

eyes were teary. "Thank you again for coming. It's nice to be able to talk with someone who really knew him."

"Of course."

Before long, our mugs were filled with dark coffee, and I had a plate of piping hot bacon in front of me. Jane wanted to know everything about Ton's life since he'd left Utah, how we'd become Rough Riders, what our training was like. I told her everything I could. I told her about our boxing, how we'd sprung Evangelina from prison, how I'd fallen for Carmen, and how Ton had saved my life. And I told her how Ton felt about her.

"I remember one night in San Antonio during training," I said. "A friend of Ton's had written him, an Eastern buddy named Walters who'd worked on the railroads in Utah too. In the letter he mentioned that you'd left town not long after Ton had. That you'd gone on a Church mission to Europe. Ton found that to be quite admirable, and he talked at length about your time together, how deeply he'd connected with you, how he hoped that perhaps someday you'd meet again at a time when it'd be easier to consider a life together."

Jane looked past me, through a window out toward the ranchland. "My father was tough-minded and rigid, but a good man. I like to think that he would've come around to accepting the idea of me marrying a Gentile one day. But after everything with Ton, I needed to get away. I applied for a mission placement in Sweden. My father died in the spring of 1897, while I was away. Ton passed a year later. I guess we just ran out of time."

We talked for a couple of hours, more perhaps than I'd talked in total over the previous couple months.

"I suppose I should get going," I said finally.

She showed me to the door.

"You must write," Jane said. "I'd love to hear how things go for you in California."

"I will."

***

In California, I found several acres of land, a few miles from the ocean, sitting on the largely unsettled Rancho Palos Verdes. The land was sun-filled and lush, hilly and fertile, with citrus groves and room for vegetable gardens. It had a workable three-room ranch house along with a small stable.

At first, the dividends from the Lewishon mine and my modest savings sustained me. In time, the land did. I lived simply, and had enough money to send some back to my mom.

Still, the fog hovered. Some nights I'd wake up in cold sweats, anxious and scared. Or in the middle of the day I might suddenly feel waves of what felt like impending doom, and they'd stick with me for some time. Many times I wondered if I could go on at all. I'd written to Jane and in turn our monthly letters became that which I looked forward to most.

She filled me in on the activity at her ranch, how the cattle were doing, how she'd come up with a new way to keep coyotes out, how the latest batch of sage that she'd planted was getting on. She'd tell me all about the books she was reading. They stretched the gamut, from Doyle to Alcott, Cooper to Dickens, Dostoevsky to Thoreau. I tried to keep up, but she read like no one I'd ever known. She loved to ask about California and the plot of land I'd settled on.

I didn't let on too much about my melancholy, but I expected she knew. Instead, I'd describe the farm's hills and groves, day-to-day life, the health of the crops. A time or two I did tell her about my night terrors, about waking up in cold sweats. And I let her know how much I cherished our letters.

Around the one-year mark, my head started to clear. I began to enjoy the rhythms of life in the groves and went into town here and there, to grab a lunch or talk to a local about farming. I started taking morning walks through the groves and surrounding hills. Pretty soon I was jumping rope and doing push-ups. I even bought some canvas to make a punching bag packed with old rags and sand and dirt. Before long, I was putting on the old boxing gloves Ton had bequeathed me and working that bag over. When my sweat got going good and my endorphins were firing, I'd think of the night I beat Piazza, about how Ton had picked me up and held me high, hootin' and hollerin', telling me over and over again, "Atta boy, Rory Mac, atta boy."

As the months rolled on, the dividends from Ton's investment in Lewishon's mine continued to grow. Between that and the citrus and vegetables, I was able to buy more land and plant more groves. All the while, Jane and I continued to write. We mailed each other books. She sent me a proper Stetson hat for the fields. I sent her souvenir cards of California so she could get a sense of what it looked like.

It took a while, but about the time my old colonel, Teddy Roosevelt, became president, I started thinking about sharing my life with someone again. That spring, I decided to go see Jane.

I boarded a car at the Los Angeles Terminal and then hired a carriage to carry me close to the Nevada line. From there, I rented out horses, stable to stable, until I reached the Union Pacific near the Utah-Nevada border.

Upon arriving in Salt Lake, I went straight to the Witherspoon Ranch. Dusk approached, the last vestiges of sunlight bounced off the snow-dusted hills. Having started up the slight rise leading to the house, I stepped through the ranch entryway, atop of which stood a wood-carved "W." Up ahead I saw Jane emerge from the stable. Our eyes met and my step quickened.

She gazed at me and tilted her body forward as if to get a good look. I waved big and started to jog to her. Well, she must've recognized the Stetson she'd bought me bouncing lightly on my head, because all of a sudden, she started quick-stepping too. We met at the cusp of the hill and embraced. I kissed her as the sun kissed us, moments before it was to dip under the horizon.

As we stood there, holding each other tight, I heard Ton tell me, "Atta boy, Rory Mac. Atta boy."

Author Bio

Carson Cunningham and his wife Christy have six kids. They live in Missouri, where Carson coaches college basketball and Christy is essentially superwoman. An earlier book Carson Cunningham wrote, *Fallen Stars*, (Nonfiction, Texas A&M University Press, Fall 2017) covers the lives and times of five American war-hero athletes who died in military service, including that of Hamilton "Ham" Fish Jr., upon whom "Ton" Fish here is based. Other works he has written include *American Hoops* (University of Nebraska Press) and *Underbelly Hoops* (Diversion Books). The Univ. of Illinois Press published a reader on the Chicago Cubs he worked on with Dr. Randy Roberts. And he self-published the *21st Century Adventures of Huckleberry Finn*.

He holds a PhD in American history from Purdue University and an MBA from DePaul University.

* For those interested in source material utilized to help draw this novel, *Alongside Hamilton*, please see the bibliographical information/footnotes in the Hamilton Fish Jr. section of Carson Cunningham's *Fallen Stars* (2017, Texas A&M Univ. Press) or feel free to contact the author.

www.ingramcontent.com/pod-product-compliance
Lightning Source LLC
Chambersburg PA
CBHW020655120726
47906CB00001B/281